GOOD
AT BLACK

GOOD DEEDS
AT BLACK PONY INN

Christine
Pullein-Thompson

RR
RAVETTE BOOKS

Phototypeset by Input Typesetting Ltd, London
Printed and bound in Great Britain
for Ravette Books Limited,
3 Glenside Estate, Star Road,
Partridge Green, Horsham,
West Sussex RH13 8RA
by Cox & Wyman Ltd,
Reading

ISBN 1 85304 231 5

One
A matter of life and death

"Gillian is going to die. Are you listening?" shouted Lisa with tears streaming down her face. "There's no hope. And she's only ten."

Lisa is the youngest in our family and much given to exaggeration. Because of this none of us believed her at first.

"Don't be silly," said my brother Ben who has fair hair. "People of ten don't just die. They go to a big hospital and are cured."

"Not always," said James who was hoping to go to university soon.

We were just home from school. We had thrown our school cases down on the kitchen table. The paying guests had had their tea and were in the garden sitting in chairs catching the evening sun. In the fields the ground was parched and dry. Our horses were in their loose boxes, because of the flies buzzing everywhere. The holidays were just around the corner waiting to be enjoyed.

"She's my best friend, she and Rosie," continued Lisa still weeping.

"How do you know she's going to die?" asked Ben.

"Everybody knows."

"That's a stupid answer."

"I heard old Forby and Miss Fletcher talking

5

about it. They said there was almost no hope. They looked very upset. They said that her only chance was to go to the United States for an operation and you know the Rosses haven't any money, everybody does. Gillian doesn't even have a father and her Mum goes out to work cleaning other people's houses for money," Lisa sobbed. "She needs a special operation, which we don't do in England, that's what Miss Fletcher said anyway."

"How much does it cost?" asked Ben slowly.

"I don't know, thousands I expect, and then there's the fare," answered Lisa wiping her eyes.

"We'll raise the money," I said.

"But how?" asked Ben.

"Exactly," agreed James.

"We could hold a raffle," suggested Lisa. And now she wasn't crying any more.

"It wouldn't make enough," replied James making tea for us all.

"A horse show then," I suggested.

"They don't make much, and supposing it rains?" asked Ben.

"It's got to be something big, really big," said James sipping tea.

"A fête, a really big one with a jumble sale as well," cried Ben triumphantly.

"With a dog show," said Lisa.

"And clear round jumping at a pound a time," I said slowly.

"And all the village involved," added James. "Because it's got to succeed."

I remember how I felt elated and afraid at the same time.

6

"What if it rains?" I asked.

"We can insure against it," Ben said.

"Too expensive," said James.

"We can have things indoors too. Things like counting the sweets in a jar," suggested Lisa.

"We need a committee," said James.

"We haven't asked our parents yet, and what about the residents?" I asked.

"They can be the committee," said James.

"They'll talk and talk. Committees are hopeless," said Ben.

"We can give Pony rides and rides in the governess cart," suggested Lisa.

"I think we need a pencil and paper," said Ben, rummaging in the case he takes to school, which is mended in the corners.

"There isn't much time. It's late already for the operation," said Lisa sniffing again.

Ben wrote FÊTE on the top of a lined piece of paper.

"We need a date," said James.

I fetched a diary which lives in the hall by the telephone. "It'll have to be a Saturday," I said.

"And not a Bank Holiday weekend," said Ben.

"And soon, or she'll die," cried Lisa.

We chose a Saturday near the end of July. I wrote down BLACK PONY INN FÊTE in large letters on the appropriate day in the diary.

"Can I tell the Rosses?" Lisa asked.

"Not yet, not until it's all decided," replied Ben.

"I'll draw the posters. I'm good at posters," said James. "I'll make them funny. I'll put dogs and horses on them and Virginia will help; she's very efficient."

Virginia is James's girlfriend. She has red hair, is rather aloof and not at all like us. She's very tidy for a start and she hates horses. I think she feels we're a bad influence on James, whom she would like to be perfectly turned out, whereas he often has his elbows out of his sweaters, and different coloured socks. But I may be wrong.

"Does she have to be on the committee?" Ben asked now.

"No. It's up to her," replied James.

We left it at that. Our parents were out. We put our mugs in the dishwasher and went outside. Our horses were looking over their loose box doors, each one so different from the others: rangy, grey Lorraine who once was mine, but now Lisa rides her; solid, tireless Solitaire who stops at nothing and is Ben's; Prince, liver chestnut with an Araby head and a brain as quick as a high-powered car, whom I've ridden for more than a year now. Our first ponies, black Limpet and skewbald Jigsaw, whom we lend to other people from time to time because we've outgrown them, greeted us over the gate with welcoming nickers. Other horses have come and gone at Black Pony Inn, but we had decided never to sell the ones we have now because they became part of the family. When I leave school I intend to train horses. I want to buy the unwanted ones and turn ugly ducklings into swans. James says that I'm mad to even consider such an occupation. Ben says it will mean I'm poor for ever. Mum believes I'll grow out of my fixation, as she calls it. But in a strange way Dad understands, for he has never wanted to be rich, only to have enough put by to live on and a little for a rainy day. He had a business once which went bust, which is why Black Pony Inn is now a guest house. When this story begins we had just four guests, two sisters called Miss Steele and Mrs Tompson and Colonel Hunter who is incredibly old and just recovered from a stroke. They are the permanent guests. There was also Captain Matthews, who liked to be called Peter.

But now we tacked up our horses before riding across the common and into the beech woods which are shady in summer, and wind-proof in winter. Soon our horses were walking like old friends under the leafy branches on the tall trees, which cast shadows like lace across our path.

We talked about the fête as we rode, imagining a fine day and a thousand people paying to come in. Lisa saw herself presenting a cheque to Mrs Ross, the joy on her face and Gillian returning from the USA miraculously cured. She started to laugh as the summer sun grew cooler and our horses hurried homewards. "We'll put posters everywhere. We'll invite the whole of my school," she cried.

"And the whole of mine," cried Ben.

"It's going to mean mountains of work," I said pushing Prince into a trot.

"But it'll be an advertisement for Black Pony Inn," said Ben. "It'll put it on the map."

"We'll need ring ropes and tents," I continued as though he had never spoken.

"And loos," shouted Lisa riding ahead.

And so the idea was born: a fête at Black Pony Inn in aid of Gillian Ross and it took off like wild fire; it didn't smoulder, it flared and raged and took over our lives until the whole house was involved and nearly all the village as well. Dad has a saying: Out of little acorns big oaks grow. And that is how it was, for from that moment the fête consumed us.

As I untacked Prince I recalled Gillian Ross; small and pale. Mum said she resembled a small bird. Her fair hair framed a thin face, her dark eyes were set back in her head, so that Ben had once alluded to them as sunken eyes, and Lisa had been furious. Her mother was a larger copy of Gillian, with the same fair hair and thin exhausted face. Had they been born that way I wondered now, or had life made them so?

And now reading my thoughts, Lisa said "Gillian will look different when she comes back cured. She's been ill for a long time, Harriet. She's been in and out of hospital, she's even been ill enough for lessons at home. The trip to the USA is really her last hope; or it could be the end for her and then her mother will die of a broken heart, because she hasn't anyone else, only Gillian."

Lisa said it with such finality that I had to believe her. Putting my tack away I remembered Gillian running round the yard with Lisa; then riding Limpet. It seemed like yesterday; but in reality it must have been months ago, if not years.

Prince was rolling now and the sun was going down behind a row of trees, and the sky was slashed with red promising another fine day. Peter's car was parked in front of the house, and

I could see Mum dishing up dinner in the kitchen. I rushed indoors to help. Washing my hands I said, "Have you heard about the fête Mum? You don't mind do you?"

"Not now, later, darling," she said.

So when we were eating pilaff sitting in the old-fashioned kitchen, while the guests rolled up their napkins and left the dining room, I said "Now we can discuss the fête, can't we? You don't mind do you? We *can* hold it here, can't we?"

And Lisa added "It's for Gillian. She's very ill."

And Ben said "It won't make a lot of mess. We'll clear everything up afterwards."

And James, who was making coffee for the guests, said "Virginia wants to help," as though her help mattered more than anything else.

Dad who had just come in and was washing his hands at the sink said "What fête?" in the maddening way he has at times.

"Not what fête! A fête," cried James exasperated.

"In aid of Gillian Ross," added Lisa once again.

"Where?" Dad asked next.

"Right here," said Ben.

"But you haven't asked me."

"That's what we're doing now Dad," I said.

"It's a matter of life and death," added Lisa.

"Do I know Gillian?" asked Dad helping himself to pilaff.

"Of course you do darling; she's been here enough times. She's the one who looks like a little bird. We can't say no darling. We must help for goodness sake, and it's my place too I'll have you remember," Mum finished glaring at Dad.

Dad held up his hands in surrender. "Yes of course. I'll help. We must save Gillian. When are you holding it? How many people do you expect? What do you want me to do? I'm game for anything," Dad said.

I fetched the diary again. Ben fetched his piece of paper. We explained the general idea. Then Mum said, "I'm not running a cake stall. I'll run a dog gymkhana."

"A dog gymkhana? Bags enter Bob," cried Lisa while Ben wrote MUM DOG GYMKHANA on his piece of paper.

"Virginia says she'll run a nearly-new clothes stall," James said.

"And we must have pony rides and pony cart rides," said Lisa.

"But we haven't got enough helpers," I cried, "because I want to run the clear round jumping and lots of other things."

"We must get the village involved, everyone, even the Rector," Mum said seriously. "How much money do we need to make?"

"Thousands," replied Lisa grandly.

"But how many thousands?" asked Mum.

"I don't know, just thousands and thousands," Lisa replied.

"We'll need judges too," I said.

"And someone on the gate," said Dad.

"And stewards to put up jumps when they fall down," added Lisa.

And now our little acorn really did seem to be growing into a most enormous oak. As we looked at each other Dad said, "We are taking on one hell of a lot."

"We can't do anything else. We've got to help Gillian, can't you see darling?" replied Mum.

"Exactly," agreed Lisa.

"And we've only got three weeks," I reminded them.

"You can move mountains in three weeks," replied Dad. "You can die or be born. You can make a fortune and lose it again. We'll work better with a deadline."

"We'll have to tell the police because of the traffic coming in and out. And arrange for an ambulance to be present," Mum said.

Two
Making plans

The next day was Saturday. After breakfast Dad called the guests together. Ben who is older than me, explained the situation. He was very diplomatic, he always is, not like James who rushes into things without thinking.

"First of all we hope you won't mind; we are not going into this idea lightly but, as Lisa will tell you, it is important and we personally feel that we should help little Gillian to recover, even if it means going to the USA." (At this moment Lisa hissed, "She's not little, she's my age.") "So we're planning a fête, which means there will be hundreds, if not thousands of people here; so if you don't agree, please speak now," Ben finished.

There was a short silence before Mrs Tomson said to her sister, Miss Steele, "We'll run an arts and crafts stall, won't we dear? We'll start knitting right away, we must help the poor mite, we really must."

Then Colonel Hunter said, "I'll run a croquet game, highest score wins a tenner, I'll give the tenner, fifty pence a go. I think I know a feller with a croquet set, great game croquet."

And I knew we had won our first battle.

"You'll judge the Dog Gymkhana, won't you Peter?" Mum asked smiling at Captain

Matthews, who replied, "It'll be a pleasure, I've got a stop-watch, if you need one, and I'll donate a cup."

We all started talking at once then. Mum explained about the dog gymkhana; "There'll be jumping, and a best trained dog class and funny classes too," she said, and I knew she was working it out as she went along.

"Virginia says we've got to have a jumble sale," James said.

"Ben and I are going to give a display in the main ring at three o'clock," I announced.

"It must be after the dog gymkhana," replied Mum.

"At four o'clock then," I suggested.

"If we have too many things, we'll get in a muddle. And that could be disastrous," said Ben.

"We'll have our arts and crafts under the cedar tree on a big table," said Miss Steele firmly.

"With a white cloth on it," added Mrs Tomson equally firmly.

"I'm afraid that will be in the way of the croquet," said Colonel Hunter. "Think again ladies."

"I'll roll the lawn for you Colonel," Peter offered, looking very much at home in patterned sweater, jeans and old trainers.

During the afternoon Ben, Lisa and I rode to the Rectory, which is small and modern and not at all as Rectories once were. The Rector is called the Reverend Leonard Smythe. According to the postmistress, because he is a Christian, he likes to be called by his christian name; so we knew if we were to make any progress we had to call him Leonard and his wife Gloria.

"Or should we call him Len?" asked Ben giggling as we rode across the common.

"No, don't be silly, that's far too familiar. But what on earth *are* we going to say?" I asked.

"Leave it to me," replied Ben trotting ahead.

Sensing our mood our horses pricked their ears and hurried. The Rectory drive was green with weeds. Leonard was washing his car. He was wearing a dog-collar under a grey shirt and grey trousers and wellies. But for the collar he might have been anyone; so that Lisa complained straight away saying, "He doesn't look at all godly, does he?"

"Shut up, he can hear you," I said halting Prince.

"What can I do for you?" asked Leonard putting down the hose he was using; then turning off a tap.

"We are on a sort of crusade," replied Ben, dismounting. "A crusade to help Gillian Ross, whom you may or may not know. And we want your blessing."

Leonard has fair hair, fair eyebrows and a small thin-lipped mouth. He looked at us now with amazement in his blue eyes. "Do I ever see you in church? Because I cannot recall your faces," he enquired without smiling.

"I knew it would be like this. I just knew it," whispered Lisa. "It's so embarrassing." (Lisa is easily embarrassed, unlike my brothers.)

"Yes, well," began Ben, before Lisa interrupted him crying, "We've come about Gillian Ross. You've got to help. We need you. She's ill and we

16

need money. Thousands of pounds. Please, please help." And now she was crying again.

"We just want your help, that's all," I added.

"She hasn't got a father," interrupted Lisa.

"And she has got to go to the USA," I continued, "because she's got to have an operation."

"Of course I'll help," replied Leonard smiling at last. "What do you want me to do?"

"Lots of things," cried Lisa.

"Manage the money," said Ben.

"Just be there," I cried.

"Will do. And I'll have prayers said for her in church, this very Sunday," promised Leonard still smiling. "Just let me know what you want nearer the time."

"Will do," said Ben turning Solitaire.

"Thanks a million," cried Lisa as we rode away. "He was lovely, wasn't he?" she continued as we trotted across the common. "I thought he would be stern, you know what I mean. But he wasn't a bit. We'll have to go to church now, because we can't not go if he's saying prayers for Gillian can we?"

When we reached home we found Mum standing in the stable yard her hands full of apple peelings for the horses. "Colonel Hunter's finally decided to leave," she told us. "He's only staying until after the fête. He wants nursing care available, and I'm not a nurse. I shall miss him terribly."

I think I had better explain that Colonel Hunter had been with us for several years, so that now he was almost part of the family.

"So we'll have to advertise for more guests,

otherwise we'll be bankrupt," Mum continued, "because Miss Steele and Mrs Tomson are already talking about moving to Oxford, so that they will be near shops and I can't blame them, can you?" she asked.

It's always like this, I thought. Always the same panic when guests leave. "What about Peter?" I enquired.

"He's only here as long as his leave lasts."

"But then we won't have anyone," cried Ben.

Mum nodded. "It'll be all right for a week or two, but after that . . ."

"We'll think of a really good advert Mum, don't despair," Ben said.

"It's the overdraft. We owe the bank quite a bit already," answered Mum feeding our horses the apple peelings each in turn. "But don't think about it for the time being, just get on with the fête."

I was already thinking about it, seeing a FOR SALE notice outside on the common, people coming to look at the house, touring the rooms, making comments. The paddocks full of bungalows, the stables converted into houses. And where would we go then? But I had heard it all before so I wasn't giving up hope, not yet anyway.

In the afternoon we went on foot to see Mrs Eastman who was chairman of the Parish Council. We took our black and white half collie, half labrador dog Bob with us. Mrs Eastman was sitting in a chair in her garden where flowers grew straight and tall and the lawn was perfect. She had a Yorkshire terrier on her knee. She was very large and the terrier was very small. We told her about Gillian and the fête. She told us that she was chairman of all the committees in the village. Ben said that ours wasn't that sort of committee; "It doesn't really have a chairman," he explained nervously.

"We just muddle along," I added.

Mrs Eastman suggested that Gillian's parents should do more for her.

"But she only has a mother," Lisa cried.

"Silly woman," said Mrs Eastman.

The sun was hot on our backs. The terrier ran round and round Bob yapping wildly, while he stood looking the other way, pretending that she didn't exist.

"We thought the Women's Institute might help. We need a cake stall you see," I suggested vaguely.

"I'll put it to them. I'll do my best," Mrs Eastman promised. "Keep in touch. I'm sure we'll do something. We won't let you down, I can promise you that."

And that was better than nothing we decided running home across the common and everything was still, and very beautiful, without a breath of wind or a cloud in the sky.

We found Miss Steele and Mrs Tomson were in the sitting room knitting socks non stop for their stall. And now we suddenly all seemed to be racing against time.

Later Mum said, "I've booked St John's Ambulance Brigade with two-way radios, a tent and an ambulance, so we'll be alright if anyone's hurt."

Dad was out. "He's seeing estate agents," Mum explained. "Just testing the water."

"What water?" I shouted anxiously.

"The property market's water," Mum replied.

"You're always on the verge of selling Black Pony Inn, but if you do I'll run away and never come back," I shouted.

"And so will I," shouted Lisa.

"The whole place needs modernizing. Guests want their own bathrooms. No one wants to share these days," Mum told us. "They ring up and ask for a room with bathroom attached and ring off when I say we haven't got one. They want a bar downstairs as well where they can drink with their buddies. Times are changing. We've been left behind, and we can't catch up because we haven't the money."

"Can't Dad do the place up himself? I'll help him," suggested Ben.

But Mum shook her head. "Nothing's settled anyway so let's get on with the fête," she said. "Put it out of your mind. Nothing is definite and we may still stay here for ever."

But I couldn't put it out of my mind, for I love all of Black Pony Inn, not just the house, but the fields too – the trees, the hedges, the wild garden which we never managed to tame; the arch above the entrance to the yard; even the old rooms above the stables which are never used because the floors are no longer safe. I couldn't imagine life anywhere else. It was unthinkable.

The next day was Sunday and Lisa and I went to church. We hadn't been for ages. Everybody looked at us as we walked in and we kept losing our way in the prayer book. Then, as we reached the sermon, Bob barged his way in and sat down at the end or our pew, and now Lisa couldn't stop giggling. But later, official prayers for Gillian were said. I prayed for Black Pony Inn to be saved. Afterwards, when we stood outside in the sunshine, we apologized for Bob's appearance but Leonard only laughed saying that it was all right because he was wearing a dog-collar. So walking home, we agreed that Leonard was indeed lovely.

"And the prayers were lovely too. I just wish Mrs Ross had been there to hear them," Lisa added.

"I expect Leonard will call on her now," I suggested. But Lisa said that she would slam the door in his face.

"But why?" I asked.

"Because she's that sort of woman. She hates vicars and doctors, and schoolteachers. She hates nearly everyone," Lisa told me. "She only likes poor people, down and outs, unmarried mothers, squatters, those sort of people."

"Poor Gillian, where is she now?" I asked.

"In hospital. Having medicines which don't do any good," replied Lisa.

"How do you know?" I asked.

"Because I keep my ear to the ground," replied Lisa looking at me defiantly as though I might not believe her. "If you want to know, when you were cleaning your tack the other day, I went and saw Mrs Ross. She told me that Gillian was in hospital and I told her that we would be raising the money needed for the operation. She didn't believe me of course. She kept on about the government. Then she said that it was sweet of us to try anyway and, though she knew we could never make enough, she appreciated our good-will. But we will make enough won't we Harriet? We've got to."

"We can only try," I said. "But thousands of pounds is an awful lot of money."

"Let's have a box for donations. Leonard can sit by it in his dog-collar," suggested Lisa. "Then everyone will know it's legal."

"Yes, we can use a vacant table. We can stick a notice on it saying, *Donations to the Gillian Ross Fund*," I said slowly.

"And rich people will put in pounds and pounds," cried Lisa.

"We need a photograph of Gillian. We can blow it up, a really nice one. You'll have to get it Lisa," I said.

And now I was seeing hordes of rich people pushing five pound notes into a collecting box, while Leonard bowed his head in thanks. I was seeing the end of the day, the money growing in front of our eyes as we counted it. Then my mind switched to an airport, to a jumbo jet waiting on the tarmac, to us waving and waving as Gillian disappeared into a departure lounge on her way to the operation which would save her life. But I knew I was going too fast. I was seeing the end before the beginning, for the race had hardly begun, and there was nothing to say we would win it. "Nothing is that easy," I said to Lisa now. "We can't guarantee anything. We can only try and try and keep on trying."

"And hope and pray," replied Lisa as we reached home.

22

Three
Riding without reins

Next day we returned to school, bearing posters made by James which read SUMMER FÊTE in aid of THE GILLIAN ROSS FUND – Stalls, Dog Gymkhana, Pony Rides, Displays and lots more – Entrance 50p. Children and OAPs 25p. There was a drawing of a horse in one corner and a dog in the other. The horse had wobbly hocks and thick tendons, and the dog looked like Bob. Almost at once, someone pointed out that there was no place or date on my poster, both of which I then added in ink.

"It's not the final one," I said defensively. "It's just for the last three days at school."

"I suppose your looney brother did it," said someone. I always wonder why people call James looney. Eccentric, inspired, out of the ordinary, untidy, looking like a poet – but not looney, surely? Now I said, "I haven't got a looney brother. If you're alluding to James, he can't be looney, because he's off to University in the autumn so just shut up will you."

"Well, only he would forget the day and place," said someone else.

Several teachers said that they would put the date in their diaries. One offered me some bric-à-brac, another offered plants. A third, called Mrs Cooke, suggested a car boot sale.

"We've got the room, but not enough people to help," I said.

"But I will organise the whole thing," she said gazing at me through pink rimmed glasses. "I know Gillian and I want to do something. All right?"

"All right," I agreed wondering what Ben and Lisa would say, because Ben has often compared Mrs Cooke to an insect which has just emerged from beneath a stone.

Several first years wanted to know more about the dog gymkhana, and I promised that there would be schedules in the village shops and the pet shop in the town. And now the fête seemed to be growing very fast. We had put TEAS on the posters, but who would dispense them I wondered, waiting for the bus home. And where would the cups and saucers come from, and wouldn't we need soft drinks too and what about ice creams? Ben was with his friends and ignored me as he always does when he's with them. The sun beat down on the tarmac melting the tar. My case was so full it wouldn't shut. I seemed to be the only person standing alone in the hot sunshine. They must think I'm looney, too, I thought glumly, looking at my bitten nails and ink-stained fingers.

I told the others about Mrs Cooke later when we were eating doughnuts in the kitchen.

"Oh no, not Mrs Cooke, she's such a drip," exclaimed Ben.

"No she isn't, not if she's going to help, she can't be," cried Lisa.

"Exactly," I replied.

Then Mum appeared with the dog gymkhana schedule typed out.

"Peter's been rolling the lawn and the croquet set has arrived and he's going to set it up for Colonel Hunter. He is a poppet. I'm going to have entries on the day for the dog gymkhana and use raffle tickets. Okay?" she asked. We nodded in unison.

"We'll do the same for the clear round jumping," Ben said.

"Mrs Eastman rang when you were out," Mum continued. "She says you can hire chairs, tables and crockery from the village hall. She sounded really nice. She's looking for more helpers. I think she's a sweetie."

"You're very complimentary today," said Ben. "Dad says that he'll get a float," Mum continued ignoring Ben.

"What's a float?" asked Lisa.

"Money, change, people must have change," Mum said. "Mrs Tomson says she will serve soft drinks and ice creams and what about a raffle? We'll need some prizes, won't we?"

"We hadn't thought about the raffle. Perhaps Leonard will give a prayer book," suggested Ben smiling in a silly way.

"Don't be so objectionable Ben," Mum said glaring. "We must get cracking; there are only nineteen days left."

"I've got to work on my display with Ben. We haven't even decided what we're doing yet," I said and I must have sounded desperate because Mum said, "Not to worry darling. Peter will give a raffle prize and Colonel Hunter, and Dad can get one from his employers and we can try Roy, your vet and the Health Centre. No one can decently refuse, not for Gillian. It's such a worthy cause."

Ben and I spent the evening working on our display. We agreed to use only Solitaire and I suggested that I would do a jumping display afterwards without any tack on Prince, not even a halter.

Then we decided where the ring would be and that spectators would enter through the arch to the stables. We decided to ask James to make signs to *Croquet Competition, Bric-à-Brac, Teas* and so on.

"Cardboard arrows," Ben said tacking up Solitaire whom Peter had ridden earlier and was not pleased to be working again. There were flies everywhere now and the earth seemed to be crying out for rain and turned to dust under our feet, while the grass was parched and yellow. I marked out a ring with stones while Ben tried vaulting on and falling off. He vaulted onto Solitaire over his tail. Then he took off his saddle and rode bareback.

"I want to jump him over fire," Ben said. "We'll have to dig a trench."

"Isn't fire dangerous?" I asked.

"Not if we're careful."

"But it's so dry everywhere," I said. I watched Ben, praying that it would rain soon, as long as it wasn't on the day of the fête.

I soon realised that Ben simply wanted me

26

there to watch and to shout things like, "that's lovely. Perfect, smashing." He also wanted me to pick up the things he dropped – the balls he was attempting to juggle with, the bucket of water which always seemed to be empty. I was no part of the display. It was solely his. "I'm going to tack up Prince," I said after twenty minutes had passed. "I'm going to practise riding without reins." Prince was marvellous, I knotted my reins and soon we were cantering with me steering him by my legs and weight alone. I only had to lean back and he would halt, to use my legs and he would turn. I stopped and stared at the sky, longing for rain because I wanted to jump, but the ground was like concrete and hard enough to ruin the toughest equine legs.

Presently we turned our horses out and fetched spades and dug a trench, our arms aching, sweat running off our faces. Supposing the others don't want the main ring here?" I asked after some time leaning on my spade.

"It's the obvious place. You come through the arch and here it is, right in front of you, and it's only a few minutes walk from the lawn and all the other attractions. There simply isn't anywhere else as good," replied Ben.

"And the dog gymkhana?"

"In the same ring. My display will be at four o'clock followed by yours," Ben told me.

"If it rains this trench will be full of water," I said a moment later.

"We'll put something over it," Ben said.

We went indoors and found Lisa cleaning the harness in the kitchen.

"We'll have to take Jigsaw out for a drive. We must get him fit," she said virtuously.

"What just for cart rides?" asked Ben.

Lisa nodded. "We don't want him to get harness sores," she said.

"We can use him to fetch things from the village hall then," suggested Ben.

"We haven't got enough people. I had a nightmare last night. I was doing everything. It was awful. I just couldn't do it all," Lisa told us rubbing saddle soap into breeching straps. "And Bob won all the prizes. I've been jumping him. He's terrific. I'll show you later," she said.

There was a new batch of posters on the kitchen table ready to be put up. The horses' hocks were better and this time the date and place had been included. The dog gymkhana schedule was there too. It read something like this: Class 1 – Jumping for dogs under sixteen inches. Class 2 – Open jumping. Class 3 – High jump. Class 4 – Best trained dog. Class 5 – Bun race. Class 6 – Best veteran. Class 7 – Consolation Race. Class 8 – Dog most like his owner.

"Mum's been to the pet shop. They're donating prizes," Lisa told us. "And Dad's been offered £50 if we agree to a double glazing stand and demonstration, whatever that means."

"The fête's growing so big, it's frightening," I said.

"I know, but it's still not big enough to make thousands is it?" asked Lisa sadly.

"I think that Cold Snap Double Glazing should pay £100 for a stand," Ben said. "Dad never pushes hard enough."

28

So Black Pony Inn suddenly became a place of seething activity; even the air seemed full of plans, until the whole house vibrated with them. Mrs Tomson and Miss Steele were still working, making things like knitted hot-water bottle covers. The Women's Institute had telephoned to say that they would run a cake stall. James had written out an advertisement for the local paper. Mrs Eastman had telephoned again to say that her niece would help with the pony rides; various other people had called offering to help. Suddenly we seemed to be meeting the village properly for the first time. People we had never known before appeared saying that they had produce they would like to contribute. Mr Brind, a local farmer, offered us bales of straw for seats around the ring. The coalman offered a bag of coal as a raffle prize, the butcher promised a joint of beef.

Soon we couldn't step outside the gate without someone calling "How's it going? Do you need anything? Can we help?" Overnight we seemed to have become part of a village we had hardly noticed before. Even Peter's aunt appeared with a pile of books in a carrier bag. "They're for the book stall," she said, though we hadn't planned one.

So school ended. It rained. Ben put newspaper in the trench we had dug, then lit it and we jumped our horses over it without much difficulty. Gillian was sent home again from hospital and we saw her sitting in her small council house garden looking pale and weak.

The lawn looked like green satin now. Mrs Eastman came to coffee and admired it. The fête was to start at 1 p.m. and end at 6 p.m. Dad had booked an ice cream van. Mrs Eastman told us that the local Brownies would serve teas, since Gillian had once been a Brownie. Mrs Cooke arrived to discuss the car boot sale and went away to obtain permission to hold it on the common. The posters were everywhere. James started to make arrows. Two of them said LOO. Fortunately we have four loos, one just inside, another outside and two more upstairs. Peter brought Union Jacks to hang over the gate. Ben practised his act over and over again. Mum screamed at him for riding without a hat. "It's not riding, it's an act," retorted Ben. "It's not the same. I don't have to wear a hat Mum."

"I don't care what it is. I won't have you riding without a hard hat; you're setting a bad example," shouted Mum.

"I'm going to be a clown. And clowns don't wear riding hats," yelled Ben furiously.

"You can wear a crash helmet then and something over it. Do you want to hit your head and be ga-ga for the rest of your life," stormed Mum.

"Ga-ga isn't a word. One is subnormal or mentally retarted," replied Ben, while Solitaire pawed the ground impatiently, smelling of sweaty horse.

I went to the tack room and fetched our one and only crash helmet, which fits us all.

"There you are. You can put a clown hat over it," said Mum turning away as I gave the helmet to Ben. "That's a good compromise."

"She spoils everything," said Ben rebelliously.

"Now you are being foul," I answered.

It's hard to describe the next few days. It rained and rained. The lawn grew soggy; the sky was permanently overcast. Our spirits were dampened. We saw a wet fête. We saw wet tablecloths and ruined cakes. We saw the fire in the trench going out, and the dogs jumping in a thunderstorm. And all the time Mrs Tomson and Miss Steele went on knitting and crocheting, so that even at meals they were working still between the courses. Lisa visited Gillian and returned depressed. "She keeps being sick," she said sitting down at the kitchen table. "And her wrists are like sticks.'

"Don't despair," replied Mum sewing rosettes for the dog gymkhana.

"I told her she would be going to the USA. I said that I wished I was going too, but I don't really, not like she is anyway," Lisa continued.

"We ought to book the flight for her," Ben said.

"We ought, but we can't," replied Mum biting cotton with her teeth.

The play room was full of jumble and bric-à-brac now. I had never seen so many used clothes before. Virginia who had a job in the day now came in the evenings to sort out things for her Nearly New Stall, which she had widely advertised without telling anyone, so that the village and surrounding area was now completely plastered with posters concerning the fête.

I schooled Prince until he would jump a course of jumps without wearing any tack at all. When he had done it, I had a bucket waiting full of goodies for him and, perhaps because of this, he seemed to enjoy his act more and more, until every time I mounted him, he made for what was to be the ring.

We harnessed Jigsaw to the governess cart and drove him round the village. We lunged Limpet and cleaned his tack ready for Pony Rides. Our repertoire of events grew as more and more people offered to help until we had everything from a croquet tournament to guess the weight of the cake competition.

Colonel Hunter spent every afternoon playing croquet alone, because no one had time to play with him. Mum and Dad had made a course of jumps for the dog gymkhana including a brush fence with laurel in it, and a gate. The event was to be judged under BSJA rules. Bob could now jump four feet and looked a certain winner of the high jump competition. Meanwhile Ben and I worked on the clear round course to be held in the bottom field. I hammered my right thumb with a hammer and it turned blue. We were permanently soaked to the skin.

Dad saw the police about putting up GO SLOW notices by the entrance on the day.

Then without warning, the skies cleared and the sun shone, raising our spirits once again until anything seemed possible even raising thousands of pounds in one afternoon.

But life is like the weather or so Mum always says, wet and fine. And as usual she was right, because suddenly everything started to go wrong.

Four
Worse things happen at sea

A day later, I woke to hear the sound of hoofs below my window. I leapt out of bed and drawing back the curtains saw that it was still dark outside. We had left our horses in what we call the long paddock. Fenced by rails it has a gate leading into the front field where the fête was to be held, and a gate leading into the bottom field, where the clear round jumping course was set up. Now I ran downstairs and unbolted the back door. Bob joined me, barking wildly, waking up the whole house in spite of my frantic cries of "Quiet, shut up Bob, be quiet". And soon I could see lights going on behind me and hear doors slamming. Another second and Lisa and Ben appeared pulling on dressing gowns as they ran.

"Is it burglars? What is it?" shouted Lisa.

"I think it's loose horses," I cried pulling on my boots, before switching on an outside light; while Ben, ever practical, shouted, "We need halters and a torch."

"And oats," added Lisa.

And now Colonel Hunter appeared on the stairs looking like an old hound and carrying a blunderbuss. "What is it? Burglars? I wasn't asleep. I never miss a thing," he said.

"No, it's horses, nothing to worry about. Take it easy," Ben said soothingly before grabbing a torch as we dashed outside. The gravel at the front of the house was covered with hoof prints. A second later we found Prince calmly grazing the lawn, while Solitaire tucked into cabbages on the vegetable plot and Lorraine stood in a flower border eating roses.

"Don't run. Go slowly. Talk to them," advised Ben shining his torch on Solitaire.

"I'll get headcollars and some oats," said Lisa running towards the stables, then falling over something and shouting, "Owh! Owh! Oh my poor knees! Damn, damn, damn."

In the distance a train raced towards London, its windows lit up. I examined the lawn by the light of Ben's torch.

"They've ruined it. Oh God, what are we going to do?" I cried.

"Repair it," said Ben.

"Just like that?"

Ben nodded. But I knew we couldn't and already I was imagining the despair when daylight broke. I saw Colonel Hunter's old face crumpled with dismay and Dad furious.

"I fell over the damned wheelbarrow," said Lisa returning with three headcollars.

When Solitaire saw us approaching, he whirled round and cantered across the lawn, giving absurd bucks and idiotic snorts while my spirits sank lower and lower and Lisa started to shout, "Catch him Ben, he's ruining the lawn for God's sake. Do something Ben."

I slipped a headcollar over Prince's ears. But

even at the best of times, Solitaire can be difficult to catch and now under-exercised because we had spent all our time organizing the fête, he bucked and zoomed across the lawn as though we were playing a game. And Ben just stood there saying, "Whoa, steady, there's a good boy."

I led Prince round the edge of the lawn. Then Lisa caught Lorraine, who followed us with half a rose hanging out of her mouth. And all the time I was thinking, this will break Colonel Hunter's heart. Bob followed us, and now the way was lit up by lights which seemed to be shining from every window in the house.

Then Solitaire flew past us with one final buck of defiance, which sent clods of lawn flying into the air.

"Everyone's going to be so angry. How on earth did they get out? Who left the gate open?" wailed Lisa.

Now our eyes had become accustomed to the dark, it was easier to see beyond the house, and besides, dawn was almost with us, so that birds were already beginning to sing and there were pale streaks appearing in the sky; and that feeling of emptiness and a new beginning which belong to the early hours.

"There won't be any croquet, that's a fact," said Ben as Solitaire clattered into the yard giving a succession of piercing snorts, and Limpet and Jigsaw neighed an anxious welcome from the schooling paddock.

"I wish day would never break because I don't want Colonel Hunter to see the lawn. I can't bear it. Supposing he cries?" I asked.

"Old soldiers never cry," said Ben.

"They'll all be furious," cried Lisa.

"And what about Peter who's rolled it again and again?" asked Ben.

"And *croquet match* is on the posters," I continued.

"And in the newspaper," added Ben.

"So we can't cancel it," yelled Lisa.

We put Lorraine and Prince in their loose boxes. Then Solitaire rushed into his looking for food in his manger, while Ben slammed the door shut after him.

Utterly crestfallen we returned indoors to Mum and Dad in the kitchen.

"The horses were out weren't they?" asked Dad accusingly as we took off our boots.

Ben nodded while Mum handed us mugs of tea.

"I fell over the wheelbarrow and now my pyjamas are stuck to my knee by blood," Lisa said.

"Come here, let me look," cried Mum.

"Yes, they've wrecked the lawn," said Ben at the same moment; while a guilty Bob watched us with his tail down and pleading eyes, fearing that he had caused the disaster.

"How did they get out?" asked Dad.

"We haven't looked yet," Ben replied.

No one was angry. I think the situation seemed too bad for anger. I'm sure we were all thinking the same thing – poor Colonel Hunter.

"It's enough to give the poor old boy a heart attack," said Dad at last.

"Don't," cried Mum fetching sticking plaster for Lisa's knee.

"We'll start repairing the lawn at first light. I don't feel like going back to bed anyway," said Ben. "We can buy new turf, can't we Dad?"

"Yes, but it won't be good enough for a croquet lawn. New turf takes months to settle," replied Dad.

While we talked the sky grew lighter. Soon we were fetching spades and rakes, and the heavy roller from behind the old potting shed. We banged down the churned and pitted turf with spades and flattened it. We added new earth where necessary and rolled it in. The sun rose; the chorus of bird song grew louder. Soon we could hear the hum of distant traffic which meant people were on their way to work. Later, when Colonel Hunter looked at the lawn, he seemed quite calm.

"I've seen worse things at sea. It'll do," he said.

"Are you sure?" asked Ben anxiously.

"Well if people don't like the look of it, they needn't play," Colonel Hunter said. "It's not the end of the world, is it?"

We returned to the stables. The long field's gate was open. Either we had left it open, or one of the horses had learned to undo the catch. We decided that in future we would tie it shut with a headcollar rope. Then we found the horses had been in the ring. The dog gymkhana's brush fence had had all its laurel removed and scattered. The gate had been trampled on. I cut more laurel while Ben repaired the gate. Solitaire's huge hoofmarks were everywhere.

When we went in for breakfast Mum was serving the guests, helped by James. A bright sun shone through the windows lighting up the dust which was everywhere.

"There's only a week left," Ben said stretching his arms. "How will we manage when it's all over?"

"Well, there's three horse shows in August," I said.

"And pair jumping at two of them," added Lisa happily.

"And there's a hundred mile ride in September which I'm thinking about," said Ben.

Then I remembered that Black Pony Inn might be on the market by then. We might even have moved. I imagined it empty, Colonel Hunter's room with its windows wide open and spiders' webs in the corners. I saw the stables turned into a house and the yard a swimming pool and I wondered why I worried so much about the fête when there was so much else at stake.

Later that day James said, "Virginia's changed her mind, she's not running the Nearly New Clothes Stall any more. She's competing with her poodle, Sophy, instead."

"But she promised and she seemed so keen," I answered.

"I can't help it, she's made up her mind."

It seemed a blow of the first magnitude, for we had expected the stall to make at least fifty pounds because there were some antique dresses to be sold as well as lots of newer garments.

"We'll have to find someone else. I'll talk to Leonard, perhaps his wife will do it," suggested Ben.

Then a boy rang asking for me. It turned out

to be Richard who wears glasses and is musical and not my type at all.

"I want to help. What can I do? Just tell me," he said.

Ben was listening. "Tell him to bring a mate and deal with the car parking in the long meadow at fifty pence a time," he said.

Richard said that would be a pleasure and that he would come the day before to sort things out.

"He fancies you, aren't you pleased?" asked Lisa in the maddening way she has, as I replaced the receiver.

"No, not at all."

"I don't think you'll ever marry, Harriet," she said next.

"I'm not fourteen yet. Do you want me to be a child bride?" I asked. "Really, Lisa, you get crazier every day."

"She can run a dating agency when she's older and make lots and lots of money," said Ben before setting off in search of Leonard's wife.

One couldn't move in the playroom now for jumble; the pile seemed to grow every day. People kept bringing it in carrier bags. Some of it was filthy and smelt. Mum said that people should have sorted it out first.

"Supposing we're left with it all?" I asked.

"We'll take it to the tip," Mum said.

Later that day I decided to ride Prince. I rode across the common and down the old bridleway which has been there since the beginning of time. As I rode I prayed that Black Pony Inn would stay ours for ever. I prayed for new guests and new bathrooms. I forgot all about the fête and

Gillian as I rode. Suddenly all that mattered was the survival of Black Pony Inn as it was, nothing more. Prince walked with a long swinging stride, his mane flaxen against his chestnut neck, his quarters rippling with health. I couldn't imagine life without him. I knew now how lucky we were and how privileged, but it hadn't seemed like that before, for we had all worked like fiends to keep Black Pony Inn going. Now we faced failure. I rode home. Mum was showing a woman with two children the horses followed by a man with spiked hair.

"Meet my eldest daughter Harriet," she said. And then, "These are our new guests darling. The children are going to have the attic, so you won't have to move."

The children were both boys. One had the face of a weasel, the other heavier features with a large mouth. I disliked them immediately. Maybe it was my mood; maybe I would be proved wrong in the future. I fervently hoped so as I dismounted and ran up my stirrups. For hadn't I prayed for guests and here they were. So I fixed my mouth in a smile of welcome. And presently heard myself say, "I hope you enjoy your stay here and like the horses."

"He's Darren and he's Gary," Mum said patting the boys' heads.

"And we're Linda and Tony," added the man smiling.

"And this is Prince," I said smiling too.

"They're only here for three weeks," Mum explained later.

"And we need the money."

"Colonel Hunter will hate them," Ben said.

"He's leaving, so it doesn't matter," replied Mum.

Our new guests were called Stamp. They insisted on helping with the washing up and were awed by the dining room. They left their napkins on the floor and their toys all over the house. If our older guests hadn't already decided to leave, they would have left anyway. We didn't grumble, but suffered in silence. And luckily the fête took up all our spare time. But however hard one tried, one couldn't really escape the Stamps for they were like flies, always in the way buzzing. They hung around the stables making silly remarks like, "Why do you pick out their feet?" And "Why don't you cut manes with scissors?" And "Why do you call him Prince?" They were forever feeding the horses with biscuits, polos and chocolates. Soon we stopped watching television because they were always in front of the only colour set in the house. The older guests began sitting in their bedrooms to avoid the Stamps. And Colonel Hunter seemed suddenly older and more decrepit. Miss Steele and Mrs Tomson went about muttering under their breath and Dad stayed out later and later. I don't think any of us trusted the Stamps, though I couldn't have said why.

Linda Stamp smoked leaving her cigarette butts in flower pots and saucers. The children threw sweet papers down without thought, anywhere. And in a strange way I think we were all a little afraid of Tony and Linda. James said that they were simply townspeople. Lisa accused me of being a snob. Ben said that they smoked drugs

41

in their rooms and we all would be sent to prison
as a result. I tried to keep my feelings to myself;
but whatever we felt, no one could deny that in
two days the whole atmosphere of Black Pony Inn
was changed. The peace was gone. Suddenly there
wasn't a room in the house which was private
any more for the Stamps followed us everywhere
like bored dogs, and we were afraid to say, "Go
away," or "Don't come into my room unless you're
invited," because we needed their money. Life
was as bad as that.

And all the time the fête grew nearer and our
preparations more frantic. Miss Steele made Ben
a stripey bobble hat to wear over his crash
helmet. James wrote out a programme which
went like this:

BLACK PONY INN FÊTE then the date and
time
IN AID OF GILLIAN ROSS FUND – Admittance
50p
Children and OAPs 20p
MAIN RING
1 p.m. – Dog Gymkhana – Entries on the day
Judge – Captain Peter D. Matthews
4 p.m. – Display by B. Pemberton riding Solitaire
4.15 p.m. – Display by H. Pemberton riding
Prince
5 p.m. – Drawing of the raffle by Reverend Leonard and presentation of the prizes.

OTHER EVENTS
Clear Round Jumping from 1 p.m. to 5 p.m.
Rides in Pony Cart

42

Pony Rides
Croquet tournament – Front Lawn
Boot Sale – The Common 1 p.m. to 4 p.m.

OTHER STALLS AND COMPETITIONS
Guess the weight of the cake
Guess the number of sweets in jar
Arts and Craft stall
Cake stall
Jumble
Bric-à-brac
Nearly new stall
Raffle

And now it was obvious that we still hadn't enough helpers.

"We could ask the Stamps," suggested Lisa.

"But can we trust them?" I asked.

"They wouldn't do it. They only do things for money. They say the State should look after Gillian. I've heard them telling Mum so," Ben replied. "They say that they don't believe in good works and that good works are for the idle rich."

I wanted to ride. I wanted to school Prince. It was like a dull ache inside me but the fête was taking up all our time. And though I longed to disappear on Prince and to ride and ride with my lunch in my pocket and return home in the dusk, there just wasn't time. James had hired a loudspeaker system. He had also taken a job clearing up someone's garden at the other end of the village, so that now he left home at eight every morning, leaving Ben and me to serve the guests' breakfasts. I hated serving the Stamps. They wanted sauces on their table and put their knives in the marmalade instead of using the spoon provided. Ben acted the part of a waiter bowing and scraping, calling everyone Sir and Madam in a loud affected voice, while I felt like a second class citizen. Bob followed us eating spilt crumbs and bacon rind.

And now the telephone started to ring incessantly with queries about the fête.

Limpet and Jigsaw remained unexercised.

We were still woefully short of helpers.

"If Virginia hadn't let us down, Gloria could be running something else," said Ben crossly, for Gloria had offered to take on the Nearly New stall.

"We can stick a notice in the village shop saying, HELPERS NEEDED FOR FÊTE IN AID OF GILLIAN ROSS," suggested Lisa.

"And then ring round," said Ben.

"We haven't got the sweets, and we haven't made a cake, so we can drop them if we like," I said slowly.

"Exactly," agreed Ben.

Mum's probably got them organized, so stop fussing," replied Lisa. "It'll work out on the day, you'll see."

Miss Steele and Mrs Tomson were marvellous. They had run fêtes before. They bought books of raffle tickets and helped Mum sort through the jumble once again. They laughed and said that it was just like the old days.

Richard appeared one evening with a friend who was called Joseph and was tall with a chain round his neck. They paced out the parking and asked questions. They stood in the kitchen like the Stamps, talking while we were trying to get supper. James gave them coffee. Ben glowered. Later they followed me round the horses asking more questions. I wished they would go away and never return.

"You're so unromantic," Lisa said when they had gone. "Can't you see that Richard fancies you?"

I didn't answer because I didn't want to be fancied by Richard. I didn't even like him particularly. And I didn't want to grow up, not yet anyway. And I was tired of being followed.

"You're getting awfully old Harriet," Lisa said next. "Don't you think it's time you had a boyfriend?"

I threw a handful of hay at her and went indoors. And now there were only two days left until the fête. I found James listening to a weather bulletin on his radio. "It's going to be stormy over the next few days," he said.

"We'll need tents then. How much does it cost to hire a tent?" I asked.

"Hundreds," replied James.

But it was too late to hire tents whatever the cost. So we would have to weather the weather. And now we looked at each other and imagined wet jumble and sodden arts and crafts.

We decided to ignore the weather. All sorts of people had delivered raffle prizes. The village shop had sent a box of groceries, the Women's Institute a bottle of home made wine and a chocolate cake. Mrs Brind had left a dozen free-range eggs and Dad's firm were donating two double glazed windows. The local electrician had given us a television set. So suddenly everything seemed to be moving at a great speed again.

Because we were all involved, meal times became erratic, but no one complained. The Stamps even made jokes about it, or rather the same joke again and again, though I can't remember it now. Peter made bunting out of discarded jumble, found music to play over the loudspeaker system and rolled and mowed the lawn until it looked like green satin again without a hoof mark to be seen anywhere. Only the Stamps still wandered about doing nothing to help, insisting that the government should pay for Gillian's fare and treatment. "That's what they're there for," they said. They kept strange hours too, often being out for dinner and then on their return demanding snacks late at night when all the other guests were in bed. Linda usually cooked these, leaving the frying pan for someone else to wash up. Then next morning they would appear at breakfast, bleary-eyed and ravenous.

"I expect they go to a pub," Mum explained. "Some people can't exist without a regular pub life."

Mum accepted the Stamps as she accepted everyone else and never complained. One day she made a ring out of binder twine and bean poles and a smaller collecting ring. Meanwhile Ben practised being a clown rolling over and over in the yard, then turning somersaults. He put on a false nose while I stood watching, wondering how it would be on the day now a mere forty-eight hours away.

It seemed impossible now that everything would be ready in time. Later that day I tacked up Prince and rode him round the clear round jumping course with my reins knotted. He went very fast but didn't put a foot wrong. And now I felt elated and sick at the same time. Lisa was teaching Bob more and more tricks. James was marking out pitches for different stalls. Oh God, let it be fine on Saturday, I prayed. Not for us but for Gillian, please.

Meanwhile Tony Stamp, ignoring the rest of us, tinkered with his ancient car which was so rusty we all wondered whether it had ever had a valid MOT; Gary and Darren watched television, while Linda sat smoking in the kitchen making Mum's eyes water. And you could almost feel the tension building up with nerves racing to breaking point. Without realizing it, I think we were all waiting for someone to start screaming, like you wait for a storm when the sky is heavy with dark clouds and you seem to be gasping for breath. Looking at Tony Stamp, I think we all knew he was wrong somewhere. But Mum said that he had paid for three weeks in advance in cash, so we couldn't turn them out. She kept saying, "It's only for two weeks now." But if it hadn't been for the fête, I think they would have seemed the longest days of my life. I had started to spend all my time now outside, dodging the two boys. The attic rooms were still strewn with clothes and toys, so that Peggy our help threatened to leave. And though the Stamps continued to ply our horses with titbits, they were still suspicious of Tony, as though they too knew that he wasn't quite genuine. And all the time Ben and I were working non-stop on our two displays, which still weren't perfect. We were both keyed up and our horses knew it, which didn't help.

To comfort us Lisa kept saying, "Nothing matters except the money for Gillian. We simply need the people to come in. Stop fussing." But I couldn't, for now my nights were scary with nightmares, when Solitaire rolled on Ben and the Stamps set fire to the house and then stood shouting, "It doesn't matter. The insurance will pay up."

Five
"I wish it was over"

The day before the fête it rained. I cleaned Prince's tack and our one and only set of harness yet again. Lisa cleaned Limpet's tack. Everyone was depressed. James disappeared to see Virginia. Dad went to work. Ben practised his act over and over again, growing wetter and wetter. Twice he fell off. Three times I had to catch Solitaire.

"You're hopeless. Give it up," I suggested.

"Bad rehearsal, good performance," replied Ben vaulting onto Solitaire's wet back once again then sliding off over his tail, then vaulting on again and juggling with balls. He was wearing ordinary clothes and scowling and I've never seen anyone look less like a clown than he did. The yard was full of puddles now. When we went indoors Mum was putting the raffle prizes on the hall table.

"What if someone steals them?" asked Lisa.

"We'll put Leonard next to them," Mum said. "He'll stop them."

"You mean God will," replied Lisa.

Miss Steele and Mrs Tomson were still working, producing more and more lacy mats. Suddenly I wished we could call them by their christian names, which were Irene and Helen. But, like Colonel Hunter, they belonged to another age when to use a Christian name was to be familiar, so we went on calling them Miss, Mrs and Colonel.

Soon Lisa and I went outside again to measure the clear round jumping course. We had agreed that two foot six (76 centimetres) was high enough and that no one would be allowed to go round more than twice. Mum had ordered fifty rosettes which were red and had CLEAR ROUND printed on them. Now Lisa started to do sums in her head. "If there are a hundred entries we'll have fifty pounds," she said, "and two hundred, a hundred pounds."

"Well done," I cried, "but there won't be that many because no one will come far just for clear round jumping," I answered.

And now suddenly I was depressed. I imagined a car park with no cars in it and Leonard sitting all day waiting for donations which weren't given. I imagined telling Mrs Ross that we had failed. I imagined again the wet cakes and soggy arts and crafts, and piles of wet jumble heaped in the playroom. Then, worst of all, I imagined Gillian getting worse.

"God didn't listen to us. We went to all that trouble and prayed in church and he just didn't listen. I can't believe it, I really can't," cried Lisa as though God was some sort of social worker sitting in an office sifting through appeals saying yes to this one and no to that one.

"Give him time," I answered.

"But look at the sky," cried Lisa dramatically. "Just look. I can't believe it, Harriet, I really can't. I mean why did we bother?"

"There's still tonight and tomorrow morning," I answered staring up at the dark sky which glowered above us, overbearing and immovable.

"I mean you try and help and then this happens," cried Lisa. "It just isn't fair and what about Leonard? He's a rector after all. He must have some influence surely."

"You've got it all wrong Lisa," I said. "Go away and read the Bible."

"Oh Harriet, you're just like everyone else – defeatist," cried Lisa.

"Me defeatist? What about you?" I shouted back, "I'm not moaning, it's you."

At this moment James returned from seeing Virginia. "The forecast isn't hopeful, but we can't cancel," he said as though we didn't know. "Mum says we can move most of it indoors. Of course the croquet will be a wash-out, and the dog gymkhana will be wet, but never mind, we'll still make a few pounds."

"But not enough. A few pounds is no good, we've got to make thousands James," insisted Lisa, "or didn't I tell you?"

The telephone ran all evening. There were people enquiring about the clear round jumping, about the dog gymkhana, about the croquet match.

A large couple appeared in a van with a load of jumble. They called everyone "Dear" and hoped we would save "the little darling". We were all on edge by this time and their jumble smelt of pig muck and Jeyes fluid evenly mixed. "We'll be there tomorrow," they promised on leaving. "We'll be bringing our lurcher dogs. Lovely dogs,

51

they are. There won't be any better, I'm telling you that," they said.

"Virginia says lurchers fight. You had better watch it Mum," James said later.

When they had gone Mum sat sorting through the prizes from the pet shop. There was a whole heap of squeaky toys, three balls and various pretence bones and doggy chocolate drops, three brushes and a dog lead.

Ben looked at them in dismay. "Bob hates squeaky toys and you know he thinks balls are silly," he said.

"But Bob isn't going to win them, is he?" asked Mum.

"I wouldn't be too certain about that," Ben insisted.

"He'll just have to put up with what he's given then," snapped Mum. It was still raining. Ben and I put our horses in their loose boxes.

"We can dry the ponies in the morning," Ben said, "but drying all four is just too much."

He looked tired. His act still wasn't going well. Solitaire was being difficult and Ben had split his clown's trousers and though Miss Steele was mending them on her sewing machine, he was afraid they might split again at some unsuitable moment. "If they do it'll make people laugh. It won't matter. They'll think it's part of the act," I said.

"Very funny," replied Ben.

We had a fry-up for supper. Colonel Hunter was very quiet. Miss Steele and Mrs Tomson asked for a tent to be provided as though tents were waiting in lines to be hired. "You can be in the hall if it's wet. Not to worry," Mum said.

The Stamps were late for supper yet again. They said their car had broken down. Peter was having supper with his aunt. James had borrowed badges from somewhere which said *Judge* and *Steward*. Dad was still out selling double glazing and the rain was still falling as endlessly as sea breaking against rocks.

"God I wish it was over," said Ben suddenly. "I wish it was Sunday, and we didn't have to worry any more. Has anyone seen my inhaler – I think I'm getting asthma."

"It's by your bed. Just calm down. We're going to do our best. No one can do more than that," Mum said, dishing up sausages. "At least we're trying to save the poor child."

Then Richard telephoned to ask, "Is the fête still on if it's raining?"

"Of course. It's still on, whatever," I replied. "See you."

"God what a wimp," cried Lisa.

Remembering her suggestion that Richard should be my long awaited boyfriend, I made no reply.

Then Leonard rang asking, "What time do you want us tomorrow?"

"Noon, say noon," hissed Mum.

"Noon, you'll be in the house if it's raining," I replied.

"Oh thank goodness, I was going to bring a golfing umbrella," he said laughing.

"He's so jolly. Are all Rectors so jolly?" asked Ben.

"Tell him to pray," cried Lisa. "Go on, Harriet, just tell him to pray for a fine day please, is it too much to ask?"

But I had already put down the receiver. "I couldn't. He knows when he wants to pray. I can't tell him what to do," I said.

"God, you're mean," said Lisa. "Oh just forget it."

Then Dad appeared, starving, only to find that we had eaten everything. And the rain beat against the windows and found its way under the back door and left a pool in the passage.

"I'll never speak to God again if it's not fine tomorrow," Lisa said.

"That will be very nice for him. I expect he's sick of your whiney voice," replied Ben disagreeably. "I know I would if I was God."

So Lisa stormed to bed, while I slipped outside to say goodnight to Prince, who whinnied softly and didn't complain about anything. Everything smelt of the countryside, wet and leafy. I stood in the rain and shouted madly at the sky, "Stop, go away clouds, please, please. Don't spoil everything tomorrow. Just dry up." But standing in the dusk with everything so wet, there didn't seem much hope and, as I walked in, I thought perhaps it's to do with Gillian, perhaps she's doomed and there's nothing anyone can do to save her, perhaps it's fate. I wished then that I believed in God or the stars or something because at that moment as far as the fête was concerned everything seemed hopeless, with nothing except failure ahead.

Next morning I lay in bed listening to the rain

falling outside. It was seven o'clock, but as long as it was raining, there seemed no point in getting up. Then Ben appeared.

"We had better get cracking. I had a nightmare last night and then a terrible attack of asthma, and my hands have come up in a rash. Look," he said.

I didn't want to look. Ben seems so calm outwardly, but often inwardly he's in turmoil.

"They look like raw meat. Are you well enough to do your display? Shouldn't you see Doctor Jones?" I asked, looking reluctantly at his raw, red hands.

"Don't be ridiculous. Of course I'm well enough," said Ben starting to cough.

"You don't sound like it."

"I dreamt that everything blew down, then Solitaire blew away. Even the raffle prizes blew away. The television ended up in a bed of nettles and Mum cried," Ben said, making Mum's crying sound the worst thing of all.

At that moment Lisa clattered down the attic stairs shouting, "It's past seven o'clock and it's the day of the fête. Get up. It's past seven o'clock."

"If only she didn't repeat herself," complained Ben wearily.

"And as if we didn't know what day it is," I said. "We'll never make enough, you know that, don't you? A couple of hundred if we're lucky," I continued. "And that won't even buy a ticket to the USA."

"The gutters are flooding," said Ben looking out of the window. "We'll need a tractor to pull the cars out of the field. We'll have to find one, Harriet."

I nodded. I wanted to go back to sleep. I wanted to wake up and find that the fête was over. I didn't want the day to happen.

Ben went away and I dressed and went downstairs to find nearly everyone in the kitchen.

"For goodness sake it's not the end of the world. We won't be washed away," Mum was saying. "The dogs can still jump and do their tricks." But the tone of her voice belied her words.

"And the jumble's waterproof," said Ben. "And the fire in the trench will burn in spite of the rain, and people will turn up in hundreds in wellies and mackintoshes. What optimism, Mum!"

"It's only half past seven, for goodness sake. Eat a good breakfast now, because there isn't going to be time for lunch," Mum replied.

After breakfast, I put the props for my display ready outside the main ring – plastic bags stuffed with straw, three cavaletti which would have no space for a stride between them, an old door painted red white and blue, a clothes line with dusters on it and funny long pants picked out of the jumble. I would jump these obstacles each way before swinging round in the middle turning Prince on his haunches. I was praying now that Prince would be in a good mood. Then I looked at the sky and saw that there was a blue streak in the midst of the clouds and I started shouting, "It's clearing up, it's going to be a fine day." And a wild cheer went up. Then James rushed outside and started up the Land Rover and cried, "Will

56

you help me fetch the tables from the village hall, Harriet? Hurry."

And Ben started to fence off the car park with binder twine, while Dad disappeared in the car to fetch the double glazing display.

"So God did listen after all," cried Lisa as clouds slowly parted revealing a blue underneath, which spread and spread until it engulfed the whole sky.

Next Miss Steele appeared crying imperiously, "Where's my table, Harriet? I want to set it up at once. I haven't got all day."

"It's only eight-thirty, we're fetching it now," said James starting the Land Rover, while I jumped in beside him, my spirits soaring. We had difficulty in collecting the key to the village hall. The old lady who kept it, peered at us through a keyhole saying, "You're muggers, I can see that," in an ancient voice which crackled like an old record on an even older record player.

"We aren't muggers, we're the Pembertons," cried James.

"Well, I don't know you," she replied obstinately.

"You try Harriet," James said. "And hurry for God's sake."

The cottage door was on a chain now. The old lady inside wore a pinny and bedroom slippers.

"No one said anything about you fetching the key. I can't give it to just anyone and I don't know you," she said again in a querulous voice.

"We're running a fête. We're trying to make enough money to send Gillian Ross to hospital in America. Haven't you heard about it?" I asked in the kindest voice I could muster. "The Rector's helping and his wife and Mrs Eastman, and the WI. It's all right, I promise, and we have permission to hire six large tables and forty chairs and the Brownies are going to borrow the tea urn." I surprised myself by knowing so much, I must have heard it said and automatically assimilated it and now it was pouring out of me like tea from a tea-pot. The old lady undid the chain slowly. She was absolutely tiny with a mass of wild grey hair. She slowly handed me an enormous key.

"I want it back," she said. "Don't forget now. I'm responsible for it. I want it back by six o'clock."

James stood looking at his watch.

"Thank you. We'll bring it back as soon as possible, I promise we won't lose it," I answered.

We drove to the hall and started loading the tables and chairs into the Land Rover. "We'll have to make at least three journeys," James said.

How can I describe that morning? We seemed never to stop running. Lunch was forgotten. Sweat ran off our faces. Prince stood on my foot. Solitaire escaped from his box and belted round the garden churning up the gravel, then tore among the tables leaving devastation behind him, while people screamed and Ben stood helplessly laughing. Jigsaw had rolled and was covered with mud, while Limpet had rubbed his mane.

Soon James had set up his public address system and kept repeating, "One, two, three, four, testing," instead of helping with the tables. Then the Brownies arrived and took over the kitchen.

Peter patched up the lawn once again and rolled the gravel. Mum set up a minute tent she had found somewhere and put a notice outside, which read DOG GYMKHANA Secretary's Tent. And all the time the sun shone seeming like a miracle.

Richard arrived with his friend. I found them chairs to sit on and promised them that Dad would provide them with change. James had stuck up the notices which read CAR PARK, LOOS and another one which pointed to the house and said TEAS.

It was eleven-thirty now and I hadn't even combed my hair. Miss Steele and Mrs Tomson were pricing things, while the Nearly New Clothes were being put on hangers by Gloria and the cakes were arriving in tins and carrier bags and more and more arts and crafts. And now it really did seem like a dream come true.

"Hallo Harriet, where am I to be?" called Leonard arriving on his bicycle. We had put his table in front of the house. Nearby a Union Jack was flying and there was a simply enormous notice saying – GILLIAN ROSS FUND – *Please give all you can*. And a blown-up photograph of Gillian looking ill and rather pathetic.

Removing his bicycle clips, Leonard said, "Well done, well done Harriet, it's marvellous, truly marvellous."

"I didn't arrange your stand, James did," I answered. "And you've got to keep an eye on the raffle prizes as well, if you don't mind that is."

"No problems. What a lovely day," he said next looking round. "And everybody's here Harriet, practically the whole village is helping. What a triumph."

Mrs Cooke appeared next. "They won't let me have my BOOT SALE outside, they say it's common land," she wailed. "What am I to do? I asked the Parish Council and the Rector, but apparently it isn't enough."

"Who are they?" asked Leonard.

"The Meachers. They bought the Lordship last year at an auction," said Mrs Cooke. "They are upstarts, just wanting to throw their weight about."

"Come on Harriet. Hop in my car and we'll go and see them," cried Leonard.

"But . . ." I cried.

"No buts, this is urgent," replied Leonard propelling me towards his car.

The Meachers lived in a new house without a fence round it. Leonard went straight to the point. "These marvellous children at BLACK PONY INN are running a fête to raise money to save a girl called Gillian Ross who needs specialist treatment in the USA if she is to survive," he said while Mr and Mrs Meacher stood before us wearing the sort of clothes one wears in the country if one's not country, but want to be.

"What's the problem?" asked Mr Meacher who sported a large black moustache.

"You won't let Mrs Cooke hold her boot sale on the common, that's the problem," replied Leonard.

"What is a boot sale?" asked Mrs Meacher smiling.

I explained briefly about a boot sale.

"Just half a dozen cars whose owners pay four pounds to sell unwanted goods from their boots. Nothing sinful, and all in aid of a poor little girl," added Leonard smiling. "You can't say no in the circumstances can you?"

"We only wanted to be asked. We are the Lords of the Manor and it *is* our common; but okay hold it and we'll be there. When does the fête begin?" asked Mrs Meacher fluttering her long, probably false, eye-lashes at Leonard.

"One o'clock," I cried.

When I was home again, I combed my hair and washed my face and put on my best jeans and my favourite checked shirt. It was nearly half past twelve now and James was still saying, "One, two, three, four, testing."

Three dogs had arrived and Mum was sitting outside her tent waiting for entries while Peter was walking about with stop-watch and measuring stick, trying to look like a judge.

Presently Mrs Cooke erected a large notice outside on the common saying, BOOT SALE. PARK HERE. And the first cars started arriving.

I found Lisa grooming Jigsaw. Mrs Eastman's niece had arrived and was watching her in tight jeans, high boots and striped shirt. She wore her hair in a pony tail and had a short upturned nose and grey green eyes.

I groomed Limpet. Then I helped Lisa harness Jigsaw to the Governess cart.

"My legs are aching already," said Mrs

Eastman's niece. "I don't know how I'll keep going for the rest of the day, I really don't."

"What's her name Lisa?" I hissed.

"Sharon."

"Well, do you think you can manage the pony rides? Limpet's very quiet and sensible. But whoever rides must wear a hard hat. I'll get you a collection from the tack room," I told Sharon.

Riders had started to arrive already for the Clear Round Jumping. I looked round for Ben.

"Here's Rosie down from London specially," cried Lisa. "Hallo Rosie, how lovely to see you. How are you?" They threw their arms round each other's necks.

"Okay, we'll do the pony cart rides won't we Rosie?" cried Lisa a second later. "Ben can manage the Clear Round Jumping and Harriet and Sharon the Pony Rides. Oh Rosie, I'm so pleased to see you, I really am."

"I'll show you what to do," I told Sharon. "I'll mark out how far to go, just there and back and not over and over again with the same tot. And no one older than ten, because Limpet's only a little pony."

"I can't stay long, I've got friends here," Sharon said, looking round the yard, looking for Ben I thought, because everyone fancies Ben.

People were pouring into Black Pony Inn now, like swarming bees. Over the address system, James announced the fête open. Next Leonard spoke wishing everyone a nice day, then begging them to be generous for the sake of Gillian Ross.

Lisa stared at me with triumph in her eyes. "Its going to be all right. It's happening Harriet," she cried. "It's really happening. We're going to make thousands and thousands of pounds. Just look at the people arriving. I just can't believe it."

A father approached us now, clutching two little girls by the hand. "They want a ride," he said holding out a fiver.

Then Lisa remembered Bob and the dog gymkhana. "I've got to go now. Ask Harriet if you need any help Rosie," she cried vanishing into the crowd calling, "Bob, Bob, come here at once Bob," while I stood looking for Dad because I hadn't change for a fiver.

Six
"Fetch the ambulance"

The Stamps stood watching me.

"You can pay later," I said after a moment, picking up the smallest of the girls and putting her onto Limpet, then putting a hat on her head which was far too big, her feet into stirrups which wouldn't go high enough for her short pudgy legs; which had white ankle socks on them and white sandals on tiny feet. Limpet put his ears back. He had given pony rides before and hated it. I gave the girl the reins to hold. She looked at her Dad and smiled. Sharon watched me before turning to grin at Ben who was collecting money for the Clear Round Jumping. It's going to be like this all day, I thought, leading Limpet across the paddock. Sharon isn't going to help. She's going to be ogling Ben the entire afternoon. Rosie was pushing children into the governess cart. She looked hot and flustered and had tied Jigsaw to the fence. It was obvious that she needed help. I lifted the girl, who was called Natalie, off Limpet and put her down. I gave Limpet to Sharon to hold and went to help Rosie. And now there was a restless queue forming for pony rides.

Children shoved one another and complained. They tried to stroke Limpet, who put his ears back and bared his teeth. I went back to help

Sharon and up and down we went. For the next half hour I spent most of my time rushing from Jigsaw to Limpet and back again. I took money too and twice I gave the wrong change. The hats were all too big, so after a time we stopped using them. Stirrup lengths became erratic, and all the time I could feel the pressure building up. The children waited impatiently for their turn, dripping ice cream down their fronts; their parents waited with cameras to take pictures. The ponies became more and more stubborn, silently sweating in the heat. Then over the loudspeaker came the announcement: FIRST PRIZE OPEN JUMPING – BOB PEMBERTON with a time of 33 seconds, SECOND PRIZE – Patch Saunders with a time of 35 seconds, THIRD PRIZE – Tatty Smith with a time of 40 seconds. And suddenly I knew that Bob was going to win nearly all the classes, because he's that sort of dog, the sort which loves to win and loves a crowd cheering him on. How embarrassing, I thought gloomily. And Lisa will let him win and Mum won't stop him, nobody will.

Our bowls of money were filling up. A large lady said, "You're charging far too much dear. It should be 10p a ride, not fifty."

"It's all in a good cause, and we've got plenty of customers Madam," I snapped back.

"They'll go somewhere else next year, I'm warning you," she replied.

"We won't be doing this next year, because by then Gillian Ross will be well," I replied.

Ben was mending one of the clear round fences with a hammer. The sun was growing hotter, the queue for pony rides longer. Rosie looked exhausted. A father was complaining. A child was crying. Never again, I thought. Soon the loudspeaker announced that Bob Pemberton had won the Best Trained Dog Competition, with Sooty Ambrose second, and Pippa Davis third. After that there was a lull in the Clear Round Jumping and Ben joined me.

"How's it going Harriet?" he asked.

Answering for me, Sharon said, "It's chaotic Ben. It needs reorganizing."

"Rosie needs a rest. She hasn't stopped once, and she's only ten," I said. Ben took over the governess cart rides. Sharon took on the Pony Rides.

"We'll make a good team," she said smiling at Ben.

I hurried to the main ring and found Lisa red-faced and triumphant. "Bob's winning nearly everything. I just can't believe it. He's absolutely fantastic. He's won both jumping classes. He cleared four foot in the high jump – four foot Harriet!" she cried.

Grabbing her by the shoulder I shouted, "Everyone will accuse us of practising over the course beforehand. And don't you know it's bad manners to win everything at your own show?"

"It's not a show. It's a dog gymkhana," retorted Lisa. "Anyway he hasn't won everything, only nearly, so that's all right. And he's not in The Dog Most Like The Owner Competition, because he isn't like anyone. He's himself. And he won't be in the Consolation Race either, so shut up Harriet, don't spoil everything."

66

Bob looked at me and wagged his tail. His collar was sagging under the weight of the rosettes he had won, his eyes were shining with satisfaction. "He's been wandering round bowing to people," Lisa said laughing.

"In a minute you'll have to take over the Pony Rides. I've got to help Ben," I said.

"But I'm absolutely knackered," cried Lisa.

"So is Rosie, and so am I," I replied.

Drowning our voices, the loudspeaker announced that the Brownies were serving teas on the front lawn. "Why not the Cubs?" asked Lisa.

"Why not both?" I suggested.

"Actually Brownies do ride and do other things," Lisa said.

On my way back to the stable yard I ran into Dad selling raffle tickets. "It's going like a bomb. I've sold two books already," he said.

"But Dad a bomb is the last thing we need," I replied.

"And Leonard keeps getting handed cheques," Dad continued. "I do like him, I really do."

Ben had stopped the governess cart rides and was changing into his clown's costume in one of the loose boxes. Rosie was back giving pony rides. Sharon had vanished.

"Lisa will be here in a minute to help you," I told Rosie.

"Lisa's got to light the fire in the trench," shouted Ben from the loose box, "so she can't give pony rides, okay?"

"I don't mind. I like giving pony rides, and Gillian was my best friend," Rosie said.

Children were still queueing. Limpet was walking slower and slower and making ugly faces at them. Soon he started stopping, saying plainly, "I've done enough, I want my tea."

"Only ten more minutes," I shouted to the waiting children. "No more rides after you've all had one, no second rides, okay?"

A small girl started to scream, "It isn't fair. I've only had one ride and Fergy's had two," she shrieked.

A boy shouted. "I didn't want a ride anyway. I would much rather ride a bike. I want an ice cream Dad, now. Do you hear? A whopper, Dad. The biggest they've got."

The sun was hot on our backs. It seemed impossible now that we had ever feared rain.

The loudspeaker announced that Bob Pemberton had won the cup for the dog with the most points. Someone booed.

Then Richard appeared saying, "The cars are all parked, Harriet. Can I help with anything else?"

And suddenly I wanted to throw my arms around his neck and cry, "Thank you, oh thank you." Instead I asked, "Can you possibly take the money for Pony Rides and lift the children onto Limpet, because Rosie's only ten and she's exhausted."

"No problem, no hassle," replied Richard.

He had taken off his jacket and tie and his hair was rumpled. He looked quite different, not half as proper and much more fun.

"Fantastic," I said.

The Dog Gymkhana was over. I ran towards

the ring in search of Lisa. Eventually I found her on the front lawn enjoying tea served by the Brownies.

"Ben wants you to light the fire in the trench for goodness sake, didn't he tell you?" I shouted.

"No one told me. How was I to know if no one told me?" cried Lisa rushing towards the house in search of paper and matches.

I found Ben leading Solitaire out of his loose box. A military march was playing. I don't know what it was, but then I'm not very good on marches or any music come to that. Ben started to attach his false nose. It was held on by a rubber band and was pink and it changed his face completely. He had painted purple spots on his cheeks and on his hands and I had a funny feeling in my stomach now. "Okay. Are you all right?" I asked.

"Of course, what do you think?"

I looked at Prince. He pushed me with his nose. Patting his neck I thought supposing he's frightened by the crowd, the loudspeaker, or by a landscape suddenly so changed? Then James announced that the raffle would be drawn at four-thirty; also the result of the croquet tournament and the winners of the competitions.

"It's four o'clock. I'm on. Are you ready Harriet?" Ben shouted. "Oh God, what's the matter with you? You've got to help me. Remember?"

I took a last look at Prince who was now wildly digging up the straw in his box. It was obvious he didn't want Solitaire to go and leave him. And I said to him, "It's all right, take it easy," while the loudspeaker announced: "And now we have a display by that well known clown, Ben Pemberton."

And now I was running ahead of Ben who was riding bareback, his face tense and strange beneath his clown's hat. Lisa was blowing at the fire in the trench with a pair of ancient bellows. She had put on a cap which was half over her eyes, so that people thought she was part of the act and were laughing already. They were crowding round the ring ropes, small children astride their parents' shoulders. Virginia was sitting beside James in the Land Rover, Mum was selling raffle tickets and Peter was going round the stalls with his aunt in tow. At that moment everything seemed set fair. And there still wasn't a cloud in the sky.

Saying, "Walk on Solitaire," Ben rode into the ring sitting back to front, and that wasn't part of the act, we all knew that. And as I ran for the tennis balls he would soon need, my heart was pounding. Mum had stopped selling raffle tickets and was standing on tip-toe, trying to see over the heads of other spectators.

"What's he doing Harriet? I didn't know he was going to ride back to front. He is wearing a crash helmet, isn't he?" she called, her face alarmed, her hands clasped together as though in prayer.

"Yes," I yelled, though I wasn't sure, because suddenly I wasn't sure of anything any more.

The fire was burning fiercely in the trench now, while Lisa stood triumphantly waving the bellows, her face covered with smuts.

Ben leapt off Solitaire and bowed to the crowd. There was a burst of clapping before he vaulted on again over Solitaire's tail and started to canter round the ring. Next he jumped the fire both ways. Then still mounted, bowed to the crowd again before holding out his hands for the tennis balls.

Handing them to him I muttered, "Be careful, for God's sake be careful."

Ben cantered round the ring juggling with the balls, his hat slipping over his eyes now so that as he handed them back to me he said, "Damn this hat. It's far too big."

Then he halted by a chair and, lifting a pail of water, poured it over his head; and now it was plain that he was not wearing a helmet because the clown's hat clung to his hair. The crowd were cheering again now. Children were laughing, grown ups clapping. Ben's act was almost over. He bowed again. Mum unclasped her hands. Ben swung round on Solitaire's back and started to ride out, sitting back to front again. It wasn't part of his act either, because no one would have agreed to it. I ran after him as alarm spread across Mum's face. Perhaps I shouldn't have run, perhaps what happened next was all my fault. I'll never know. Some moments seem to last for ever. This was one of them. Leaving the ring Solitaire started to trot. The crowd scattered. "Steady, whoa, walk," Ben's voice sounded scared now.

I wanted to shout, "Jump off Ben," but the words died in my throat. Solitaire broke into a canter and I knew now with dreadful certainty that he was making for the stable yard. Mum was running now, her face twisted with fear. "Hang on Ben. Don't let go," she cried.

But there was nothing to hang on to, not even Solitaire's mane, because Ben was still sitting back to front. I stifled a scream which rose in my throat and ran too. Solitaire was galloping now. He gave a triumphant buck as he reached the yard. Ben's arms seemed to clutch wildly at nothing then he lay still on the cobbles, still, oh so still. While Mum screamed, "He isn't wearing a hat. I told him to wear a hard hat or a helmet. Don't you notice anything Harriet? Why are you so blind?" As if I was responsible. As if I was the eldest.

Then she was kneeling beside Ben while I caught Solitaire and with shaking hands put him in his loose box, while the loudspeaker announced: "And now we have a display by that well known local rider, Harriet Pemberton on her Wild West Bucking Broncho, Prince!"

"Fetch the ambulance. You're not riding Harriet," Mum shouted.

I ran to the Red Cross tent. Two nurses and a man were drinking tea.

"You're needed in the stable yard, my brother's had an accident," I said trying to keep my voice steady.

They leapt into the ambulance and drove through the crowd and then all sorts of people seemed to be running towards the stable yard – Dad, a large woman I didn't know, the Stamps and a man crying, "I'm a doctor. I'll deal with this."

When I reached the yard again Ben was sitting

up and saying, "What happened? Where am I? Where's Solitaire?" He was soaking wet and his face was the colour of putty. Mum was crying, "I told him to wear a hat," she sobbed.

"I thought he was, and why did he ride back to front?" I asked.

The loudspeaker was calling again. "Harriet Pemberton on Prince will now perform for your pleasure. Where are you Harriet? We're waiting."

"You're not going Harriet," cried Mum.

"But they are waiting for me," I answered. "I can't let them down Mum. They've paid to see me. I'll be careful, I promise."

"You're all the same. You never listen to me," she complained. "You all go your own way. And I have to pick up the bits."

Prince was already wearing a headcollar. I added a rope, knotting it round his neck.

"I promise I'll be careful," I repeated.

Not everyone knew that Ben had fallen off. Some people were still talking about his performance as I rode towards the ring with Prince keyed up beneath me, with a spring in his back which wouldn't go away, his head high, his ears pricked. Cameras flashed. I didn't really want to perform now. I was too worried about Ben.

"Do you want me to lead him?" asked a tall man in jeans.

I shook my head.

"He's over the top. You've just fed him oats," hissed Lisa suddenly.

The Stamps were watching. The children standing by their parents. Linda was smoking.

What were they thinking? I wondered. Why didn't they ever smile?

"I haven't fed Prince a grain of oats," I said turning to Lisa. Then I was talking to Prince, telling him everything was all right, trying to still the wild beating of my own heart, which he could feel as surely as I could feel his.

I heard Richard call, "Good luck Harriet. Don't rush it. Take your time." And he sounded years older than me now – almost grown up. I went into the ring and now my whole performance seemed an anti-climax, for Prince behaved perfectly. He knew the act better than I did. I even had time to notice Dad watching and Peter talking to his aunt and Leonard laughing. Prince cantered and changed legs, jumped everything even the fire now burning again, turned on his haunches and repeated the same performance the other way, then halted in the centre of the ring while I bowed, and then it was over and I hadn't touched the headcollar rope once, Prince had done it all himself so that the whole act seemed to have taken only seconds as I rode out of the ring to the cheers of the crowd.

The stable yard was empty. The ambulance gone, the sun setting, the fête almost over. I dismounted and Lisa appeared and said "Ben's only concussed. I'm going to jump the cross country course on Lorraine. Rosie's jumping Jigsaw. I've turned Limpet out. I need your hat for Rosie."

I handed Lisa my hat and turned Prince out and went indoors on legs which suddenly felt weak. Richard followed me.

74

"Was it a success? Did you make enough?" he asked.

"I've no idea," I answered.

"You were tremendous. What a performance," he said.

"It was Prince. He's a wonder horse," I answered. "He did it all himself."

The Stamps were making tea. They handed us each a mugful. "Ben's not in hospital then? And you seem to have done all right," Tony said.

"But it won't be enough money," I answered. "We won't have made enough. And Ben should be in hospital."

"You may be surprised," said Linda opening a packet of biscuits and offering them round, just as though the house was hers. "As for Ben, he will be right as rain by morning. He doesn't need to be in hospital, love. No way! They only take them in to safeguard themselves."

Drinking my tea I wondered who "they" were. After that Richard followed me round the stalls. Half the jumble was still there; but all the nearly new clothes had gone. The boot sale was over. James announced the number of the winning raffle ticket – "Number 105 pink." Finally Colonel Hunter appeared and was wildly cheered. Pointing to the TV, Dad said, "I'll deliver it to your room Colonel. Well done!"

Rosie won a box of chocolates. Mrs Eastman a bottle of whisky. Otherwise the prizes went to strangers.

"Thank you very much Richard, you've been wonderful. I don't know how we would have managed without you," I said.

Richard looked at me. "I'll be seeing you then. Don't work too hard," he replied and sounded disappointed.

Then I dashed upstairs and found Ben in his room with the curtains drawn. He was sitting up. "What happened? I can't remember a thing after I jumped the fire. Did I finish my act?" he asked.

Tears were running down his face.

"Yes, it was a triumph. But you should have worn a hat," I told him. "You could have been killed Ben. Why did you do it?"

"I don't know. I think I thought the crash helmet would spoil the look of the act," he replied after a time wiping his eyes.

"I expect you're meant to stay quiet for twenty-four hours," I said, moving towards the door.

"Did you fall off? How did your act go?" he asked grabbing me by the arm. "And is it over? Has everyone gone?"

He didn't want me to leave. He wanted me to stay and talk. He didn't want to be left alone. "Yes, and it's your fault, you've missed the end. You should have worn a helmet," I said ruthlessly. "And I can't leave all the clearing up to Lisa and James, and Mum and Dad, we're all exhausted and it wouldn't be fair."

"Mum was crying," Ben said, letting go of my arm. "She was sitting on the concrete. I can remember that quite clearly, sitting on the concrete and crying. I feel I've let everyone down and I should be helping clear up," he said pushing back the bedclothes.

"Stay where you are. You can't get up for hours, you've been concussed Ben. And you know what that means, don't you?" I asked. "Someone will bring you supper, but I don't know when. I'm sorry." I edged out of the room guiltily. The sun was going down beyond the stables. I was aching with hunger now. The day seemed to have lasted for ever. Bob was waiting for me, his tail wagging slowly. He knew that Ben was hurt; he always knew when things went wrong. I knelt down in front of him now saying, "It isn't your fault. You've been wonderful. You always are."

Then I heard Lisa calling, "Harriet, where are you? They're counting the money." And Mum was saying, "I've called another doctor. I thought it best. I don't want anything to go wrong with Ben. It's better to be safe than sorry." But she didn't sound certain. At that moment, like me, I don't think she was certain of anything any more.

Before I went into the kitchen, I went outside. The garden smelt of roses. The blue sky was clouding over, Mrs Eastman and Gloria were pushing unwanted jumble into black plastic bags. Colonel Hunter was sitting on the lawn looking incredibly old.

"A young whipper-snapper named Richard Catson won the tournament. Do you know him Harriet?" he asked.

I nodded slowly. "He was a helper. He deserved to win. What was the prize?" I said.

"Twenty-five pounds. A man called Meacher was second. He's not my sort, too showy," Colonel Hunter continued.

"I agree with you there. Would you like me to help you indoors?" I asked.

I found his stick. We went indoors slowly

77

together. The television he had won in the raffle
was waiting in his room. I found a cricket match
on BBC 2 and left him watching it. Everyone
had left now except for a few staunch helpers.
Virginia was listening to music with James in
his room. Miss Steele and Mrs Tomson were lying
down in theirs. The Stamps were watching television in the sitting room. Like housewives of the
future, the Brownies were still washing up in the
scullery, which some people call the utility room.

In our house the boys help with everything,
there are no divisions of labour. James lays the
tables every day for the guests. Dad can make a
good lasagne. I offered help but the Brownies
didn't need any. They were giggling and humming and pushing each other. Next I found a man
standing in the hall holding a black bag. "Black
Pony Inn?" he asked uncertainly. "I'm Doctor
Bandhi." He wasn't our usual doctor. He came
from a far away land and his English wasn't very
good. I led the way upstairs. Ben was sitting up
in bed. "I'm perfectly all right. I don't need looking at. Everyone's making a fuss about nothing,"
he said crossly. He still had paint on his face and
hands.

A minute later Mum appeared saying, "He was
concussed. He's better now. He won't have to go
to hospital will he?"

And Lisa was calling to me again. "They're
counting the money Harriet. Hurry," she shouted.

Seven
We start to crack up

I found Leonard counting money in the kitchen. He looked at home there, though the sink was full of mugs and the dishwasher full of unwashed crockery. He had been given nearly a thousand pounds in donations. The cheques were written to THE GILLIAN ROSS FUND though we hadn't yet opened an account in that name. The jumble sale had made ninety-nine pounds and three pence. The Nearly New stall fifty-six pounds and nine pence. The competitions thirty pounds, the raffle two hundred and ten pence, the boot sale twenty pounds and the croquet tournament fifteen pounds, after the prize money had been deducted. The arts and crafts had made one hundred pounds exactly. Leonard was writing it all down neatly, in a red exercise book, his dog-collar slightly askew. Lisa was sobbing. Her sobs rocked her entire body. Bob licked her hand. "It isn't thousands of pounds. It isn't even two thousand,' sobbed Lisa looking at me with tear-filled eyes.

"It's a wonderful result,' said Leonard. "It really is. You must be proud of your children, Mr Pemberton."

Mum appeared as Dad started to wash mugs. "It's a start. But I wish it were more," Dad said. "How is Ben, by the way?"

"All right, thank God. But he's got to rest of course," Mum replied. "But you do realize that so much money has never been made before, Lisa, not even at the Church Fête."

"But it isn't enough," cried Lisa. "Can't you understand? We need thousands of pounds. Anything else is chicken feed."

"But it will buy the poor girl a ticket to the USA," replied Mum. "Surely they have charities there which will help."

"Sick joke," sobbed Lisa.

Leonard put the money in a tin and stood up. "I've itemized everything. The next collection in church will be for Gillian. I've made up my mind," he said.

"It'll be too late. Time has run out," cried Lisa.

Dad saw Leonard out while Mum said, "We can make some more. We can hold something else."

"But there isn't time," replied Lisa. "I keep telling you that, why don't you listen? She needs treatment *now*. I shall sell Lorraine. I've made up my mind. She'll fetch two thousand. And we can sell Jigsaw and the governess cart, because we never have time to drive him, and the antique chest in the hall and what about the tallboy in your bedroom Mum? What is furniture after all?"

"But none of the furniture is worth thousands, Lisa. And if we got rid of it, we'd have to buy something new, and that isn't cheap either," Mum said.

"No, you wouldn't have to. You could keep your cloths in cardboard boxes under your bed. The Rosses do," replied Lisa.

"You can't sell Lorraine. She was mine first," I

shouted, "and she's too old to sell. And Jigsaw is old too. You're not selling them, Lisa, because they're not yours to sell. So just shut up will you?"

"I owned Jigsaw and then you gave me Lorraine. I shall ring *Horse and Hound* tonight. I bet they have an answer-phone," shouted Lisa. "Gillian matters. She's my best friend. Lorraine can have a nice home somewhere, she can go on living, can't you see? She won't die if she's sold. But if we don't do something, Gillian will. It's as simple as that, Harriet."

I wished that Ben was with us, Ben who has an answer to everything. The sun was going down above the trees. The day was over. Mrs Tomson and Miss Steele joined us now carrying more dirty tea cups. "What a day! And you were marvellous Harriet and so was Ben until he had his accident," Miss Steele said, smiling brightly. "And we sold all our arts and craft; there's not a thing left. Not even a needlecase. You must all be so happy."

"You were wonderful, both of you, real troupers," Mum said. "But we didn't make enough. We've got to sell a lot more to raise enough, jewellery and things. I'm selling my horse," said Lisa grandly. "She's worth at least two thousand pounds."

"How noble of you," replied Miss Steele. "Won't you miss it?"

"All the time, but that's not the point is it? I have to sell her to save Gillian. That's all that matters – Gillian," Lisa replied.

I imagined Lorraine being sold. I imagined her loose box empty. She had been mine for three wonderful years. "She isn't yours. There's nothing in writing Lisa," I said. "You didn't buy her, you just appropriated her. She's still mine. I only lent her to you."

"That's a lie, a downright lie," shouted Lisa. "She's mine. You said so. You gave her to me."

Fortunately at that moment James put his head round the door. "Virginia's left. Can you help me take the chairs and tables back to the village hall Harriet?" he asked.

I was glad to leave the kitchen. We loaded the tables and chairs into the Land Rover. "What about Ben?" asked James.

"Still concussed," I answered.

"He's mad, Lisa's mad. Sometimes I think our whole family is mad," James said starting the Land Rover, which is old and battered. "I mean Dad goes on and on making a pittance selling double glazing, and Mum doesn't charge the guests enough to make a decent profit. She should have the whole place done up and charge double. Neither of them have an ounce of business sense. And now it's too late, any fool can see that."

"Have you any business sense?" I asked climbing into the Land Rover.

"More than they have," replied James.

"I don't think they care much about money. They think happiness is more important," I answered. "Mum doesn't notice cobwebs, or chipped skirting boards, she doesn't want lots of money. She's not made that way."

"And now they haven't any," said James bitterly.

We loaded the chairs and tables into the Land

Rover and returned them to the hall. We made two more journeys, and then gave the key back to the old lady who smiled at us this time and said, "You're welcome."

"I wish you would speak to Lisa," said James as we drove homewards in the gathering darkness. "She's going on and on, and there's nothing more we can do. She'll take it better from you Harriet. She's becoming a bore. She's making us all miserable. It's bad enough having the Stamps without Lisa going on and on about Gillian; we've done our best. We didn't make Gillian ill, and we're not responsible for her. Her mother is."

"I can't influence Lisa. She wants to sell Lorraine. She wants us to sell all our valuables," I answered. "She wants to be a martyr."

"I suppose I can see her point," replied James slowly, "but by the time we've done it, Gillian could be dead."

I was so tired now that my eyes would hardly stay open any more. We parked the Land Rover in the yard. There was paper scattered everywhere. It didn't look like our yard any more. It looked like the beginning of a garbage heap.

"We can clear up tomorrow," James said switching off the engine. "God what a day! I shall be glad to get away from here. It's getting me down. I'm sick of waiting on everyone. I'm sick of being the guests' 'dear boy'. I want to be free."

We walked indoors together. Lisa was talking into the telephone. She was saying, "This is Lisa Pemberton speaking. I want to put in an advertisement. It is: Grey Mare. 14.1, 12 years old. Excellent jumper. Ideal for Pony Club events.

£2,000 to good home only." Then she turned to me and said, "I'm putting it on *Horse and Hound*'s answering service. I've said Good Home Only."

And I wanted to scream suddenly. Everything seemed to be falling apart. Lisa was selling Lorraine and James wanted to be free. I sat down in the hall and burst into tears. James made me a cup of tea. Mum put her arms around me. "You're exhausted, darling, that's what it is. It's been a long day. You'll be better in the morning," she said.

"No I won't. I'll be worse. Lisa's selling Lorraine. Can't you see Mum, everyone's going mad?" I cried. "We all are. There's Ben talking gibberish upstairs and you walking about in an exhausted state, looking like a zombie and the guests getting more and more peculiar every day. What's happening to us Mum? That's what I want to know."

"You're tired," Mum repeated.

"And if Gillian dies, Lisa will never get over it," I continued remembering her organizing funerals for small birds which had fallen out of nests. The weeping and the wailing when anything died. "And if she sells Lorraine, I'll never forgive her, not as long as I live. And what about Black Pony Inn? Are you selling it?"

"I don't know where to hide the money. Any suggestions?" asked Dad appearing, with a tin full of money in his hand.

"Put it under the sofa cushions," James answered.

"In our bedroom where we can guard it," Mum suggested.

"We'll have to go to church tomorrow because Leonard helped. We can't let Leonard down," said Lisa joining us, looking smug because she felt that she alone was doing the right thing.

"I'll never speak to you again if you sell Lorraine," I shouted, glaring at her.

"Please don't quarrel," begged Mum. "We're all so tired; everything will look different in the morning."

I was crying again now. And Dad was laying the table for the guests sitting in their places already in the dining room, waiting for a meal. Mum looked like a tired elf. We had been on our feet for thirteen hours and were all exhausted. And dinner was two hours late, though no one had complained.

Later sitting down at the kitchen table I said, "I don't want to go to church tomorrow, because I always lose my way in the service. Do you mind if I stay at home? God doesn't seem to be helping much, does he?"

"I lose my way too. They keep changing the order. It doesn't matter. The thing is to go," Mum answered. "And God doesn't help you just like that."

Next door Miss Steele was humming a hymn. James made a face in her direction and said, "Silly old fool."

"Don't say that. Just don't, that's all," Mum told him.

"Virginia says this is an old people's home," retorted James.

"It's kept you," Dad replied.

"Virginia's father's a solicitor. They have

plenty of money," James answered smugly. "And a big house."

"Not as big as ours, and they don't have horses," I said.

"I don't ride anyway," James replied.

We seemed to be cracking up. We seemed to have reached what people call a watershed in our lives. We were beginning to break up like ice breaks, starting at the edges. If Ben had been there he would have diffused the situation. But Ben wasn't there. He was upstairs in a darkened room. And now like dogs, when one snarls, another snarls and another and another, so that now I turned to Lisa and cried, "I mean what I say! If you sell Lorraine, I'll never speak to you again. I'll never help you with your homework or discuss anything with you. I won't lend you dresses either or make-up, or anything."

"Your dresses aren't worth borrowing, and you haven't any make-up," Lisa answered smiling. "Besides I'm doing it for Gillian, not for myself. I'm selling Lorraine for Gillian. What's wrong with that for God's sake? Doesn't her life matter? Don't any of you care?"

Mum shut the door between the kitchen and the dining room.

James said, "Here we go again."

I started to eat and all I could taste were my tears falling into the food. The guests were silent in the dining room. I guessed that they were trying to hear our words and then except for the Stamps they would shake their old heads and say, "Listen to the young. They haven't any manners nowadays. If they had grown up in the war like

86

we did, they would be different." Peter had gone out to dinner, so now it *did* seem like an old people's home and suddenly I could see James' point of view. But I hated it coming second hand from Virginia; somehow that made it seem like poison.

Later Mum said, "Lisa's asleep upstairs fully dressed. I don't think she will wake up for hours."

Dad was still worrying about the money. We should have had a safe but because our permanent guests always paid by cheque, we had never needed one until now.

"People will know we have it here. So we've got to be viligant," Dad insisted.

We all made suggestions. I said, "Put it under your pillow, Dad, and have Bob in your room for the night and lock the door."

James suggested the cellar. Mum suggested he put it under some loose floorboards. But in the end I didn't know where he put it. I was just glad that Lisa wasn't there to insist that we pay Mrs Ross first thing in the morning because with so much of the money in cheques and everything having to be accounted for, it might be days before we could give her anything at all. Later I went outside to say goodnight to the horses. Everything was marvellously still now with a dark sky full of stars. The scattered paper lying everywhere looked like flakes of snow. Success seemed so near and yet so far. It seemed near because the fête had been a tremendous success, but far because we still needed thousands of pounds. I imagined Gillian lying in a hospital bed. She was the same age as Lisa and always ill. It seemed so unfair.

Dad was locking up. "You were wonderful Harriet. You all were. I feel so proud of you," he said, putting an arm around my shoulders.

"But we didn't make enough and it will haunt me for ever," I replied.

I lay in bed and everything was quiet and empty and sad, because we had failed. My mind went backwards and forwards over the day's events. I kept seeing Richard tousled and helpful. He had been so nice. I would ask him round I thought. Lisa was right. I was growing older and older; it was time I had a boyfriend. I would enter Prince for the Cross Country next weekend in Lord Lester's Park. I would put Gillian out of my mind. But what would we do with all the money, I wondered. Surely donations would have to go back if Gillian died? And then I slept at last.

Next morning I rose early and fed our horses. A mist lay over the yard. Bob followed me. There was no sign of anyone else. I made tea for Mum and Dad and took it upstairs. Miss Steele was in the bathroom. Ben was recovered and shouted, "What about me? Where's my tea?" So I went downstairs and fetched him tea in his favourite mug, and went upstairs with it, and sat on his bed.

"Sunday, church," he said. "I suppose I'll have to wear a tie."

"I'm going riding after lunch. I'm going to enter Prince in the cross country next weekend. It's only two foot nine," I told him. I wanted to forget the fête and Gillian. I wanted to forget all about money and the future.

"You'll have to wear a dress," said Ben smiling.

"What for?"

"Church of course."

The service was at ten o'clock. We filed in all together, Lisa wearing an absurd hat and gloves, "Because God would like her to," she said.

Miss Steele and Mrs Tomson came with us. But not Ben. The congregation, already assembled, stared as we entered. We filled three pews in the old grey church. Leonard said prayers for Gillian. Lisa sobbed and I could hear Bob barking outside the church door. I was wearing a dress I had had for two years. It was too short and too tight.

We shook Leonard's hand as we left. He held mine for ages murmuring "Well done Harriet, well done."

We hurried home to the Sunday papers and mugs of tea.

"What are we going to do with the money we've got? Are we taking it to Mrs Ross now?" asked Lisa blowing her nose.

"Not just like that. We have to pay it in and account for it properly," Dad said.

"Can't I even take them a hundred pounds, just to cheer them up, to give them hope?" demanded Lisa.

"Not yet. We must do it legally," replied Dad.

In the afternoon Lisa and I rode through the woods; then across a field just cleared of hay. Lisa said that she would compete in the cross country event before she finally sold Lorraine. "Then if I win some money, I'll give it to the Rosses," she said.

I wanted to say, "Supposing Gillian doesn't live that long," but I didn't. People waved to us now as we crossed the common. Even Mr Meacher shouted, "Hi there," and then something silly about fair girls on grey horses. We seemed to have made a great many friends in a very short time and now the bells were ringing for the evening service.

Then we heard Ben calling, "Harriet, Lisa where are you? There's good news. Really good news. Hurry."

I pushed Prince into a canter while Lisa shouted, "What's happened? What is it? Is it about Gillian?"

"Yes, hurry. Gallop." yelled Ben. "It's great, terrific."

And as I galloped I remembered that Ben was supposed to be keeping quiet for another twenty-four hours and I yelled, "Go back to bed. You're supposed to be resting."

Eight
Too late!

Everybody seemed to be waiting for us in the yard.

"The *Echo* rang," Ben said.

"The *Echo*? What's that?" cried Lisa dismounting, her face suddenly scarlet with hope.

"The newspaper of course," Ben said.

"They are taking over the appeal," James added quickly.

"They are arriving to interview us tomorrow morning," Ben continued as though James had never spoken. "They are going to make a feature of it."

"The awful Mr Meacher put them up to it. Apparently he owns it," James said.

For a moment everything seemed to be going round and round. I leaned against Prince. I just can't believe it," I said.

"Nor can I," said Ben.

We turned our horses out in a daze. I imagined Gillian catching a plane. I imagined her returning cured.

"I hated Mr Meacher. I feel awful about it now," I said.

"It will increase his sales, so you don't need to. It's an emotive story, which is just what he wants," James answered.

"Exactly," agreed Ben.

I watched Prince roll. So the fête wasn't in vain after all. It was like a snowball, which started rolling; and gradually grew bigger and bigger, gathering more and more money as it rolled along. And we had given it the first push.

When we rushed indoors Mum was singing in the kitchen. "Isn't it wonderful? I'm so happy," she cried.

"I want to tell Gillian's Mum, right away," Lisa said.

"We'll drive round to her place. It will do Jigsaw good to have some exercise," suggested Ben.

We harnessed Jigsaw, who was glad to be working and pushed his head into the cellar. Lisa was singing now. Ben was whistling. Bob followed us out onto the common. James had already gone to tell Virginia the good news.

"She will be so thrilled," he had shouted, leaping onto his bike, then pedalling away like a mad man.

"I can't wait to see Mrs Ross's face," cried Lisa as we bowled along in the governess cart feeling like people of long ago. All around us the gardens smelt of new mown grass. The sky was blue and everything seemed lit with hope.

"It's our prayers, our prayers have been answered," cried Lisa dramatically a minute later. "And I'm so happy."

Jigsaw's ears were pricked in front of us. The harness gleamed, his hoofs were quick and cheerful on the road, while on the common people were walking their dogs, gleefully, because of the sunshine.

"I hope we can settle down after this. I'm sick of constant pressure," said Ben.

"You sound like an old man already," complained Lisa.

I looked at Ben's sore hands and knew what he meant, and thought he should still be resting.

Gillian and her mother live in the last house in a row of council cottages built at the beginning of the Fifties. When we reached them, Lisa, who was driving, threw the reins at me and, leaping to the ground cried, "Bags tell her the good news."

"Lisa gets madder every day," complained Ben.

"She cares desperately," I answered.

"Perhaps she'll be a social worker when she grows up," suggested Ben. "She can drive other people mad then."

The Ross's house was the shabbiest in the row. Everything needed painting. There was a broken window stuffed with cardboard and the tiny front garden was full of weeds. The front door was scratched and battered and the chimney stack askew. Then I saw that the curtains were drawn across all the windows. Lisa banged on the door while Bob barked, and a cat retreated to the top of a tree in the next garden.

"She isn't there. Look the curtains are drawn, that means Gillian's dead, doesn't it?" shrieked Lisa. "People draw curtains when there's a death in the house, don't they?"

"They did years ago, but not now. You got that out of a book," replied Ben in a practical voice, though I knew that he was worried too.

Ben and Lisa walked round the house and banged on the kitchen door. Bob barked. They banged again and again until Ben said, "There's no one here. They're out."

"What are we going to do then?" asked Lisa in a frantic voice.

"Go home," said Ben. "And just remember 'Too late' are the saddest words in the English language," he added bitterly.

"But we've got to find them," cried Lisa. "They can't both be dead. We've got to know the truth."

"But not here, they're not here," replied Ben getting into the governess cart.

"So we're too late. I feel it in my bones," said Lisa. "I feel death all about me. It's the end, isn't it?"

"Oh do shut up," I said. "Nothing is certain. We don't have to give up just like that. Mrs Ross may be out shopping. She may have forgotten about the curtains. She may be like James and not notice such things."

"But it's Sunday," cried Lisa before a voice called, "Are you looking for Mrs Ross?" And we saw a tall, thin woman with tangled hair which reached to her shoulders.

"That's right," said Ben. "We have some good news for her."

"Well, her little girl took a turn for the worse last night. She's in Intensive Care. Her Mum's in the hospital with her. I can't tell you any more," the woman said.

"What time was that?" I asked because suddenly it seemed important to know.

"Yesterday about ten o'clock. She called a taxi.

She looked terrible. So distressed. I'm feeding their cat," the woman said.

"Thank you for telling us," said Ben glumly.

We turned Jigsaw round and drove home.

"So we are too late," cried Lisa with awful certainty in her voice.

"All that for nothing. What will we do with the money if they've flitted?" asked Ben.

"You're both crazy. Why should she be dead for goodness sake?" I asked taking the harness off Jigsaw.

"She may be recovering. There *are* miracles you know."

"But not enough to fly to America. You have to be well to fly to America," insisted Lisa.

"Not that well," said Ben.

We left Lisa with her arms round Lorraine crying into her mane. Mum rang the hospital but no one would tell her anything. "Apparently they'll only talk to close relatives," she said gloomily.

Then she rang Mr Meacher.

"Everything is in hand. We have a reporter at the hospital. If she dies we will still run the story – rather differently of course," he said. We were all listening and he sounded unconcerned; as though whether Gillian died or not was immaterial. It was the story which mattered.

"Is she dying then?" Mum asked.

"No she's in Intensive Care, that's all I can say," replied Mr Meacher.

I don't think any of us slept much that night. Ben and I met in the kitchen at two o'clock in the morning and made ourselves cucumber sandwiches.

"I'll look a wreck for the press," I said.

"It doesn't matter, nothing really matters compared to death," replied Ben.

"What's actually wrong with Gillian?" I asked next.

"Something with a long name; something so rare that no one has ever done the operation before," Ben replied.

Soon dawn was breaking, heralding another day. But would Gillian ever be better, I wondered, creeping back to bed. And as I crept, I saw that Mrs Tomson's light was on and wondered whether she too was worrying. I could hear Mum and Dad talking. I longed for morning then and news, as you long for water when you're thirsty. I wanted everything settled one way or the other. Then Lisa appeared and sitting on the end of my bed said, "I can't sleep."

"I can see that," I answered.

"There's no need to be horrible," Lisa retorted. "We are living through a terrible time, a life may be hovering between life and death at this very minute. It's awful. And what about Black Pony Inn?"

"Whatever happens we'll have to go on," I said.

"Right to the end," said Lisa. "But to what end? We've been so lucky, we have had so much and she's never had anything. I mean we've had a lovely house and horses and a Mum and Dad, and plenty to eat; poor Gillian had free school lunches and everyone knew and sneered at her. She had

96

clothes from Oxfam too. And her satchel was held together by safety pins."

Outside the birds were singing fit to burst their lungs. Then the milk trolley arrived and there was a rattling of milk bottles below my window and Bob barked. It was all wonderfully normal. "I want to stay like this for ever, in this house, with Mum and Dad and you and Ben and James. I don't want things to change," I cried.

"You're mad," cried Lisa. "You can't stop progress. You can't stop growing. Do you want to be a dwarf?"

"I can't be a dwarf because I'm five foot already," I said. "And another thing," I added, "I don't want Lorraine to go, not ever."

"But an advertisement will be out tomorrow. I telephoned the *Echo*. They had an ansaphone too," Lisa said, not looking at me. "So we may get some calls quite soon."

"I shall slam down the receiver then; and I don't want you on my bed a minute longer, because I hate you," I shouted. "Go away, go on, go, because you know we can't sell Lorraine. She's too old to start a new life. It isn't fair."

"She's only twelve. That isn't old. I'm being unselfish that's all," replied Lisa bursting into tears.

Nine
"Please go away"

So next day Lisa and I were not on speaking terms. She rose early and at eight o'clock went in search of Gillian's mother. At ten minutes past eight the telephone rang. I picked up the receiver, my heart hammering. "I've rung up about the advertisement in the *Echo*," a voice said.

I hesitated then I said, "I'm sorry the mare's sold," and put down the receiver. "Who was that?" Mum called from the kitchen.

"Nothing. Wrong number," I lied.

Two minutes later it rang again. "This is Mrs Carr," a voice said. "I saw your advertisement. Can we see Lorraine this morning?"

"Sorry, she's sold," I answered putting down the receiver once more.

"Another wrong number," I said.

"Perhaps we should complain; there must be a fault somewhere," Dad said scrambling eggs. "But why don't you have breakfast instead of standing near the telephone like a lost soul."

"I *am* a lost soul," I answered. "And I can't leave the telephone because Lisa's selling Lorraine."

"Already?" asked Mum.

"Yes, already."

"I'll speak to her," Mum said without enthusiasm.

"It's too late. Lorraine's advertised in the *Echo*. Life's a nightmare; but she's not selling Lorraine because I love her just as much as I love Prince. I shan't let her," I shouted.

"Well we can't keep all the ponies for ever. It isn't fair on them," Mum said, trying to be neutral. "Besides the future is rather bleak just now."

I took the receiver off the hook and went outside. Lorraine and Prince were waiting at the gate to be let in. Flies hovered around their eyes. A breeze stirred the trees.

I counted the years we had had Lorraine. It came to five. I saw her going away and never returning. I saw her growing old. I saw her tethered on waste land, neglected, unloved, for once you've sold a horse anything can happen. All sane people know that. And even if Lorraine was sold, two thousand pounds might not be needed, because the readers of the *Echo* might donate enough. So it's all mights I thought. Life seems made up of them, and, if onlys. And I wished that Dad was a solicitor or a doctor. Just someone with a large safe income coming in every year.

Then a lady appeared with three children and waving madly ran across the yard towards me crying, "We've parked outside. I hope that's all right. You see I'm not much good at turning with a trailer hitched on the back. My husband can manage, but I can't. We saw your mare advertised. We've seen her at Pony Club rallies. We rushed straight here, because we wanted to be first. You see we know we want her. She's still here, isn't she? She hasn't been sold yet, has she?"

I looked at them while my heart sank down as far as a heart can go. I said, "Yes, well," to gain time. But now they were leaning over Lorraine's door talking to her, their pockets bulging with titbits. Dressed in riding clothes, the lady was slim with long hair and the three children looked as though they were roughly nine, eleven and twelve years old – just right for Lorraine.

"Will she have to live alone?" I asked to gain time to think.

"Goodness no. We would never keep an animal on its own. By the way, the name's Wallace. You must have seen us at rallies. I'm Trudy and the kids are Lucy, Emma and Giles."

It was a perfect home, anyone could see that.

"Can we try her?" she asked next, obviously puzzled by my lack of enthusiasm.

Like a sleepwalker I fetched Lorraine's tack and watched them put it on.

"I'll ride her first," said Trudy, mounting easily, before riding into the nearest paddock.

"She's lovely, I do love greys, don't you?" exclaimed Lucy.

"We've always wanted her," said Emma.

Giles was playing with Bob, throwing a stick for him to fetch.

It was eight forty-five now. Soon Ben must appear I decided and wished he would hurry. Trudy dismounted and helped Lucy onto Lorraine. I started to cry and, because of that, I rushed into the tack room and shut the door after me, and now all around me was the wonderful smell of saddlesoap. I said to myself then, "Think of something Harriet, you fool, go on, think. Don't give up without a fight."

Then I thought of Gillian and now I didn't know what to do. I thought that life was full of choices and whichever one chose one would be filled with remorse afterwards. I thought, if I turn the Wallaces away, Lisa may sell Lorraine to someone ten times worse, and what if Black Pony Inn is sold? Doesn't that make a difference? But at last Ben appeared. "So there you are," he said opening the tack room door. "What's going on?"

"They want to buy Lorraine," I told him. "They've always wanted her. They're terribly nice, and I don't know what to do."

"We must stall," said Ben. "We must say we have ten other prospective buyers lined up. We must play for time."

"But that's a lie about the buyers."

"Sometimes one has to lie," Ben said.

"I feel so guilty," I said. "They're so nice. I don't want to let them down."

"It's Lisa's fault. Not yours," Ben replied. "By the way, did you take the telephone off the hook?"

I nodded miserably.

"You are a fool. Someone might ring to say that Gillian's better, which would solve everything," he told me.

"Oh Ben, what a hope," I answered.

"While there's life there's hope and for goodness sake wipe your eyes and stop being an idiot. All is not lost," Ben said.

"But even if the Wallaces don't buy Lorraine, people will go on ringing up. Lorraine is so well known, there will be dozens of them," I moaned wiping my eyes with a stable rubber.

There was a knock on the tack room door. Ben opened it. Trudy Wallace stood outside smiling.

"We love her. We want to buy her. We don't even want her vetted," she said as though she was doing us a favour, almost as though we should be grateful that she was offering to buy Lorraine. I stifled a sob, which I tried to make sound like a hiccup. She took a cheque book out of an expensive handbag. "It's two thousand pounds, isn't it?" she asked.

"Thank you very much, but we have many other prospective buyers appearing throughout the day," said Ben sounding rather pompous. "So we can't say yes until this evening; but if we do sell her, we promise that she will go to you."

"What do you mean, *if*? And who are the prospective buyers? I'm ready to write out a cheque this minute," said Trudy Wallace.

"That nothing is final."

"But she was advertised."

"I know. My sister Lisa wants to sell her and give the money to the Gillian Ross appeal," explained Ben.

"The Gillian Ross appeal?"

"It'll be in the *Echo* tomorrow morning. You'll know all about it soon enough," replied Ben wearily.

"I still don't understand."

I was crying now; the tears cascading down my cheeks in an unstoppable flood. "Please go away," I sobbed. "I'll write to you. I'll explain everything in a letter. I'm just terribly sorry."

102

"The kids will be broken-hearted. They had set their heart on the mare. They'll be crying all the way home," replied Trudy crossly. "You can't do this to people, it isn't fair and it's dishonest, totally dishonest."

"But not illegal. It happens with houses all the time. You think you can buy one and then you can't," replied Ben.

Trudy called to her children, "Come on. They seem to be crazy here. I don't know what's going on," she said. Then they all walked out of the yard without another word.

"Damn everything," I said. Then, "Why do these things happen to us Ben? It's so horrible, I can't bear it and I hate letting people down."

Lisa appeared then whistling, with Bob at her heels.

"I've been to see Mrs Ross. Gillian is out of Intensive Care. She's very grateful. I told her I was selling Lorraine," she said. "Who were those people here by the way Harriet?" she added.

"They were looking for somewhere else. They thought we were a riding school," I lied.

"That's right and super, great, well done Lisa," Ben told her, his voice full of bitter sarcasm. "You must be feeling terrific, a real martyr. *Girl sells horse to save friend* – what a headline! Just right for the *Echo*. Perhaps it'll even make the national press, think of that Lisa, your photo in *The Times*."

"Don't be so beastly Ben. You know I'm not doing it for fame," replied Lisa calmly. "I'm doing it for Gillian, that's all. I shall miss Lorraine all the time. I shall miss her for ever and ever. I shall cry myself to sleep."

I went indoors and ate breakfast. I didn't taste it. Mum looked distraught. Colonel Hunter was feeling ill. The toast was burnt and the scrambled eggs had stuck to their pan. Worse, our help Peggy had failed to show up, and Twinkle, Lisa's cat, had stolen the bacon. It wasn't Mum's morning, anyone could see that.

"Peter's leaving today; and Miss Steele and Mrs Tomson were talking about moving to Oxford soon. I think they're tired of burnt toast and late meals. And we haven't anyone else booked in," Mum said.

"You can enjoy a well-earned rest, then Mum. People will turn up, they always do," Ben said.

"More oldies, or mad children, or the dregs of broken marriages, or people like the Stamps to drive us mad," Mum replied. "We can't go on like this. We'll have to have less horses. They are not earning their keep. Perhaps it's a good thing Lisa's selling Lorraine, because we'll have to cut down sooner or later. It's inevitable."

I knew then that we should have let Lorraine be sold, because it would have been one less horse to feed through another winter, and one fewer set of shoes ever six weeks. Silently I made some more toast. Then I took a breakfast tray up to Colonel Hunter. The sun was shining again. We should have been happy. Why weren't we, I wondered? Why were we always quarrelling? What was happening to us? I helped Mum clean the house while Ben shook the mats and went round with a cobweb brush, removing spiders. We were sitting in the kitchen enjoying mugs of tea when the press arrived in the shape of one girl and a photographer. They introduced themselves as Paul and Caroline. Caroline was wearing a checked shirt and jeans.

"We're from the *Echo*. We want to make the Gillian Ross appeal a big splash. It's going to be our lead story," she said. Paul wore jeans too and a T-shirt.

Ben fetched Lisa and James. I should have felt excited, but I didn't. Too much had happened. Too much seemed to have been said already. I felt like someone who has tried to climb a mountain, and returned without reaching the summit. I wished I had not cried in front of Trudy Wallace. I felt a failure with a capital F. And I couldn't think of anything to say to the press. Anyway Lisa did most of the talking, which was only fair because Gillian was *her* friend. Unfortunately we failed to stop her saying that she was selling Lorraine to raise more money for the fund. I made a face at her, and Ben kicked her foot but she just continued talking and we could all see that she was enjoying being the centre of attention, and for some reason that made it seem much worse.

But at last, the talking was over and the photography began, the main picture being of Lisa with her arms around Lorraine; and we all knew what the caption would be for that one: FOR SALE TO SAVE A FRIEND. I felt frozen inside now. Ben wouldn't look at me. James was in a hurry because he had arranged to spend the morning with Virginia and the morning was fast disappearing. Mum wanted to finish the cleaning. Finally Caroline asked us about Black Pony Inn.

"We may as well get you some more business. You certainly look as though you could do with it," she said.

"So Mum told her about the set up. She sounded tired and disheartened. Then Paul photographed the house. "A little free publicity," he said as though handing us a present. Then they both got into their car which had *Morning Echo* written across it in red, and drove away with Caroline waving out of a window.

"They were great weren't they?" asked Lisa. "And we won't have any trouble selling Lorraine now will we?"

"I just thank God it's over because they're sure to misquote us," James said.

"The whole piece will be hotted up and emotive. It has to be."

"Will it be on the front page?" asked Lisa happily.

"More likely to be the middle spread," replied James, who has a friend on the local paper.

"I won't read it. I don't even want to see it. I hated them; they were so condescending. We don't look as though we need business, and it's an insult to suggest we do," I cried.

"But it's true," said Mum quietly. "We are not making money, anyone can see that. If things don't improve soon we'll have to sell up, lock stock and barrel."

"Not yet," I cried. "Not until next year. Not now."

Mum nodded. "I keep telling you so. The bank

106

won't lend us any more money, it's as simple as that," she said.

"But there must be something we can do . . ." my voice tailed off.

"Not the horses as well?" asked Ben.

"I don't know. We haven't decided anything yet. It's still in the balance, but time is running out, because you can't run a guest house without guests and the place is getting shabby, or haven't you noticed?" asked Mum. "Where will we go?" asked Lisa.

"Somewhere smaller," Mum said. "I'm sorry, but that's life. I kept warning you. We simply can't go on any longer with all the horses and the huge garden and no one to clean the windows or the gutters. I've reached the end of my tether."

Tethers again, I thought furiously. God how I hate tethers.

"We must go on fighting. We must never give up," insisted Ben wiping tears from his eyes.

"We've lost the battle, can't you understand?" cried Mum. "Your Dad and I have tried and tried to make things work. Do you think he likes selling double glazing? Do you think I like having Linda Stamp dropping cigarette ash in the soup? We may be grown-ups, but we have feelings too, you know."

Only a year ago we had been in the same state. Then a film company had rescued us using Black Pony Inn as a film set, paying us thousands of pounds. Now we were in the same state again and it was too awful to contemplate. But this time I had the feeling it really was going to happen and it seemed so unfair when we had spent so much time trying to save Gillian Ross and we were to lose Black Pony Inn. That was the cruellest blow of all.

Ten
A gift straight from heaven

I spent the afternoon trying to forget what Mum
had said. I jumped our cross country course on
Prince and once again he went beautifully. Peter
had checked out at mid-day saying, "Duty calls.
It's been wonderful here. But now it's back to the
regiment and Germany."

He had kissed Mum goodbye and shaken Dad's
hand. Mum had turned away without a word,
while Dad had stood in the drive waving him
goodbye. In the evening I groomed Prince for ages
and I couldn't help thinking, next year he may
be gone, they may all be gone. We may be living
in a small modern house with just Bob for company. And I wondered what I would do all day
without any horses.

Later that evening Mr Meacher rang. I answered the telephone. "Is that Harriet?" he asked
and without waiting for my reply said, "I thought
you would like to know that the little girl is sitting up and taking food. The crisis seems over for
the time being and the appeal opens tomorrow
with a centre-page spread. There's a lot of local
interest already and we hope to reach our target
within forty-eight hours. I think it will make

national news, so don't be surprised if radio and TV news contact you."

I tried to sound interested, but really at that moment I could only think of Black Pony Inn being put up for sale. It had eclipsed everything else.

"So, Harriet, you're going to be news whether you like it or not, because it's a heart-warming story which shows the young in a new light, as carers rather than vandals. And that's what everybody likes to hear." Mr Meacher continued.

"I'm so glad Mr Meacher. Thank you for calling," I replied slowly. "It's great, really great." I put down the receiver and rushed into the kitchen. "Mr Meacher thinks the appeal will raise enough money for Gillian to go to the USA in forty-eight hours. Aren't you going to cheer?" I cried.

"Terrific," said Mum.

"Another nightmare over," exclaimed James.

"I will bike into town first thing and get a copy," Ben said.

"It's like a dream come true," said Lisa. "Will Gillian see the paper?"

"I don't see why not," replied Mum.

"And I hated Mr Meacher. I thought he was a phoney," said James.

"Perhaps we can turn Black Pony Inn into a home for the elderly, now," I suggested looking at Mum who was making a cup of Ovaltine for Colonel Hunter, who was already in bed. "I quite like elderly people."

"The Wrinklies you mean," said Ben.

"But we're not qualified. You need to be a nurse," Mum said.

"And I suppose you need fire escapes and wheelchairs, and lifts," Ben added.

"We could hire a nurse and change the place," I suggested slowly. "It would be better than leaving, wouldn't it? I don't mind sleeping in the cellar, if only we can stay Mum."

"Oh Harriet," Mum cried putting her arms around me. "It may not happen, it's just a possibility. Anyway life changes and one has to put up with it. Life was never meant to be a picnic. You may even like living somewhere else."

"Something will happen," Ben said. "Don't jump your fences until you come to them Harriet. Something will turn up."

"I think I've heard that somewhere before," I said.

Bob followed me outside. The sun was setting above the common. Soon the summer would be over. I saw the leaves falling off the trees, the apples ripe in the orchard, the hedges festooned with blackberries. I saw Black Pony Inn with new people moving in. The old pump removed from the kitchen, the bread oven turned into an alcove with a light inside. I saw someone else sleeping in my bedroom and the fields sold one by one for development. I saw the trees in the orchard falling into the long grass, and the stables being converted into a house. I saw diggers and cranes and men with ladders. Then I saw us in a different house with a small garden and a front door bell which went ding dong. And I knew that I should be celebrating the money being raised for

Gillian, but I couldn't. Ben licked my hand. I cleaned the loose boxes ready for the morning. I swept the yard and all the time I was thinking, in a month we could be gone. Then I heard Dad calling, "Harriet. What are you doing out there? It's past your bedtime."

Bob ran ahead of me. The Stamps had gone out so Ben was watching Show Jumping on television. Mum was laying breakfast. I went up to bed and dreamed I was on a ship sailing to an unknown destination.

I was wakened next morning by Ben outside my room saying, "I've bought the *Echo*. They've got it all wrong of course. And I look awful, really ugly."

I pulled on my dressing gown and went downstairs and read the article with Ben sitting by the Aga in the kitchen. It made Black Pony Inn sound like paradise and us like ministering angels. There was a photograph of the house in colour and one of us grouped around Lorraine with a caption which read: BELOVED PONY FOR SALE TO SAVE FRIEND, just as James had forecast. Lorraine had her ears back. I was scowling, but Lisa was smiling showing off her almost perfect teeth.

"They've done us proud," said Ben. "I didn't expect colour, did you? If only I looked better, but the house looks fantastic, doesn't it? You don't even notice the crooked chimney and you can't see the cracks in the walls. It looks so old, and smart as well. It looks worth half a million at least."

"Yes it's as good as a house agent's advertisement," I said. "You know, unique property, listed grade 2,' that sort of thing."

We ate an early breakfast. Outside the flies were already buzzing, so I brought the horses in, or rather they rushed into their boxes and started munching feeds the moment I opened the gate.

It was like any other morning, except that our guests were soon leaving and the *Gillian Ross Appeal* in the *Morning Echo* had opened. And Lorraine was still for sale. And now I couldn't object, because all our other horses might be going too. I'll ring up the Wallaces later, I thought. I'll apologize for our strange behaviour. I'll say, "Of course you can have Lorraine, you're a perfect home." And the money won't have to go to the *Gillian Ross Appeal*, it will go to placate the bank which won't lend us any more. It's all quite simple if you don't think too hard, I decided. If you keep your emotions out of it and don't look back at the wonderful days you've had riding your grey mare. I thought, we'll move and Dad will go on selling double glazing and Mum will get a part time job, and they'll have the difference between Black Pony Inn and our new home stacked away in a Building Society.

I leaned over the loose box doors and looked at Prince, who had arrived unrideable and untouchable. Now he was my best friend. I could hardly bear to look at Lorraine, because I had loved her so much and still did. She was part of my life, a whole chapter of it, a part which would remain with me for ever. I spoke to dark brown Solitaire, who could out-walk all the others, and go all day without tiring. I spoke to the ponies and remembered riding Limpet for the first time when I was six, just before Mum and Dad bought Black Pony Inn.

Presently Lisa appeared. "Mr Meacher's on the telephone and there's been three other calls. Things are happening Harriet. You're not crying, are you?" she asked.

I shook my head. "Nice things or nasty?" I asked.

"They sound nice," Lisa replied.

"Where's Dad?"

"Singing."

"I bet," I said. "Why do you lie, Lisa? You always do. It's a bad habit. And what about Lorraine? Is she still for sale?"

"I don't know, and don't you try that big sister act on me Harriet," Lisa replied.

There was a feeling of autumn in the air already. A plane roared overhead. Soon Gillian might be on her way to the USA. We had started it all and so she would recover because Lisa had arrived home from school crying a few weeks ago. At that moment it should have been enough but it wasn't. I felt no triumph and my name in the *Echo* meant nothing to me. For none of it mattered compared with the possibility of losing Black Pony Inn.

"I suppose you're in one of your moods again Harriet," Lisa said.

I didn't answer.

"Breakfast Harriet," Dad called. "Hurry up, there's good news again. Run."

I walked. I still didn't believe it. I had given up

believing anyone or anything. Mum was cooking breakfast.

"Mr Meacher rang and talked for forty minutes. He's already had several thousands of pounds donated mostly from local companies. Isn't it fantastic?" she asked.

Colonel Hunter was still in bed. Recently he had seemed very old. He had stopped appearing for breakfast and now had it in his room every day. Miss Steele and Mrs Tomson were talking once again about Oxford in the dining room. It seemed like the end of an era.

"I was going to several shows," I said. "But I suppose I had better not now."

"Why not darling? What are you talking about?" asked Mum unusually pretty in a flowered dress.

"Because if we've got no guests, we won't be able to afford anything, will we?" I asked. "We'll be back to square one, no money and no hope."

"But haven't you heard? Didn't Lisa tell you darling? We've had three calls already about accommodation; and, even better, a woman who runs long distance rides wants to put up here on a regular basis," Mum said.

I stared at Mum. "But will it be enough?" I asked.

"And Mr Meacher wants to help us to improve the place," Dad said. "We haven't worked out a deal yet. But we'll probably have a swimming pool and tennis courts. We're going up in the world Harriet, so don't look so glum. Of course we've got to work things out. Mr Meacher wants to put up his business associates here. He owns lots of companies as well as the *Echo*. I think we'll even have a chef, and a waitress," finished Dad laughing.

"And so I'm not selling Lorraine after all, because they expect the fund for Gillian will be over-subscribed by lunch time," cried Lisa.

"We're going to have a celebration tonight," Dad said. "Mr Meacher has invited us to dine with him. We deserve a good meal, don't we?"

"Definitely," replied Ben appearing.

"I thought, I thought," I began but now I couldn't remember what I had thought, because a feeling of total happiness was stealing over me. Then I thought, we've won, we've won on both fronts. Maybe God has answered our prayers. Maybe it was going to happen anyway – who can tell? Only one thing is certain – if we had left Gillian to die we would have been selling Black Pony Inn by the end of the summer.

"An architect's calling later to see what we can do about the old rooms above the stables," Dad said.

"But they aren't safe; the floors have holes in them," I cried.

"Exactly. He's going to make a plan. We want them as rooms for the long distance riders, with a bathroom at one end. They'll eat in the house and sleep over the stables. They'll love it," Dad said.

"And if anyone rings up, Lorraine's no longer for sale," Ben added. "It's definite. We agreed to it five minutes ago."

In my imagination I saw everything done up; the window frames gleaming white, the old stairs to the rooms where grooms had once slept, repaired. The sound of many hoofs on the cobbles. A coming and a going which hadn't happened there for years.

"If it takes off, we'll get a girl groom to help, so you won't have to work so hard," Mum told me her arm round my shoulders, her face against mine.

"Mr Meacher may buy a couple of horses and keep them here, so you see everything's going to be all right after all," said Lisa smugly.

"And Mr Meacher wants us to stay in his villa in Corfu," Dad continued. "It's off the beaten track, and it sounds beautiful."

"I just don't believe it," I said. "So many things can't happen all at once. It isn't real. There must be a catch somewhere."

"Black Pony Inn remains ours," said Dad firmly. "The agreement is only for ten years. After that we will review the situation. It's a Godsend, Harriet, a gift straight from heaven. The solicitors are drawing up the details today. This means we're really safe at last. We needn't worry ever again."

I wasn't used to gifts straight from heaven. I couldn't believe it and still thought there must be a catch somewhere.

"And now we have to go to hospital to see Gillian," Mum said.

"What all of us?" I cried.

She nodded. "It's another publicity stunt, isn't it?" I asked.

"Yes, but in a good cause. Go and do your hair

117

and put on tidy clothes. You smell of horse Harriet. And hurry."

"But I haven't had any breakfast," I cried.

"It doesn't matter, eat something in the car," Mum said.

When we reached the hospital, we found Gillian in a private room surrounded by flowers. There were reporters in the corridor and a flustered nurse who said, "You're late and this hospital is no place for the press."

"Just look at the cards, there must be hundreds," Mum cried smiling brightly while Lisa rushed straight into the room and, throwing her arms around Gillian cried, "Oh it's so lovely to see you."

The nurse looked on disapproving. "You can't stay long. She mustn't be tired out; she's got a long journey ahead of her," she said.

We stood around Gillian's bed while lights flashed and questions were asked and answered, written down, recorded. There were tall men in sandals from TV-AM, earnest young women from the *Echo*. Lisa talked and talked. Ben smiled the polite smile which he keeps for such occasions, a smile which never reaches his eyes, which is really not a smile at all. I looked at the polished floor and thought of Black Pony Inn done up, while James picked at his finger-nails and Mum and Dad stood in the doorway holding hands. At last it was over. Gillian lay back in bed exhausted. The nurse ushered us out while Lisa waved, calling, "See you Gillian. Next stop USA."

We hurried along hospital corridors to the car park now jammed with cars.

"Well done, you were fine," Dad said.

"I don't want to be famous. I know that now. I hate the press," I said.

"I don't. I think I want to be an actress," Lisa cried running ahead.

After lunch which was cold meat and salad, Ben and I rode through the woods talking about the future.

"It's going to be different of course," Ben said. "We're going to have more time and holidays abroad like everyone else."

"Do you think the girl groom will look after our horses too?" I asked.

"I expect so. I expect Mr Meacher will pay a lot to keep his horses here. I think it's rather like winning the pools," Ben continued.

"I suppose we'll have to be a bit smarter," I said as we started to trot.

"Yes, we'll have new clothes for a start and new tack. Everything is going to be run on a different basis. I think Dad is going to be paid a huge salary to be manager. We'll probably have a licence too. We're going to be rich Harriet," said Ben grandly.

I thought of new tack, of a navy blue riding coat with a red lining which I had wanted for years and years. I imagined a horse box with a wide ramp and room for five horses. I imagined going out for the day and knowing that there was someone to look after the horses, so that we needn't hurry back.

'We'll have to change our image. We must look

successful. I expect we'll fly a flag, that sort of thing," Ben continued.

"What flag?"

"Our own flag," said Ben.

The horses caught our mood and tossed their heads and reached into their bits. The woods were cool and secret; the sun bright above us.

"You'll have to buy things for Corfu," said Ben as we turned homewards. "Suntan lotion, a bikini, dark glasses. You'll have to change a bit."

"I'm hoping to get out of going," I said. "It's not my sort of life. I'm not right for it."

But Ben just laughed and trotted on.

After that we dressed up to go out. It wasn't easy because we simply hadn't the right clothes, but we did our best.

There were cameras at the dinner too – *Mr Meacher self-made man, Newspaper baron dining with the Pembertons* that would be the caption I decided.

There was prawn cocktail or melon, followed by a huge choice of dishes, followed by something off the sweet trolley or cheese. None of us were used to eating so much and Lisa muddled up her knives. Mrs Meacher talked to me about school. She told me about her education which had been expensive and private. I tried to attend to what she was saying, but all the time I was imagining Black Pony Inn restored to its former glory with more rooms and bathrooms added, but carefully because Black Pony Inn is a listed building and cannot be spoilt. I saw new riding clothes for me and new rugs for Prince, and Lorraine growing old at peace with us. I saw worry wiped from

Mum's face for ever and Dad sitting in an office totting up the money coming in. I saw myself going out with Richard wearing new shoes and a new dress. I saw Gillian returning cured. Then I noticed Mum looking at me and saying, "You'll never have to give up your room again for guests Harriet because we're keeping the old bit of the house separate."

And everyone was standing up now, because the dinner was over. Mr Meacher kissed me and Mum goodbye. Except for the moustache, his face was smooth and smelt of after shave lotion. Dad kissed Mrs Meacher and so did James. Ben avoided kissing anyone and so did Lisa. Outside the sky was full of stars.

"What a dinner," said Ben smiling his true smile as we walked towards the car park.

"I ate too much. I had two helpings of nearly everything and now I feel sick," complained Lisa.

"We must get a better car," said Mum getting into the driving seat of our old estate car. "We must cultivate a new image. You know the saying, success breeds success. Well we must look successful from now in, all of us. No more old clothes and elbows out of sweaters. If you need something new, say so. All right?"

"Okay," I said. "But I hate being smart."

Bob welcomed us home. The horses whinnied from the paddocks. It was difficult to accept that Gillian was actually going to the USA. It just seemed too good to be true. Suddenly I seemed to have everything I had ever wanted.

But then as I climbed into bed I heard Mum

say to Dad, "Sally has left a message saying the Stamps have left. Apparently they packed their bags in a great hurry after a phone call. It sounds fishy to me." (Sally had come in to see to the guests while we were out. She's young and cheerful and very efficient, unlike Peggy our more regular help.)

"Well at least they had paid up," replied Dad. "So that's all right. We needn't worry darling, even if they didn't say goodbye."

But of course nothing is as simple as that, and the next morning we were woken by policemen hammering on the front door. There were three of them and they flashed cards at Dad, muttering police, and rushed into the house with Dad in hot pursuit still in his pyjamas crying, "What do you want? This is private property. Where's your search warrant?"

Mum followed barefoot, in her dressing gown, ringing her hands together while Bob barked and Miss Steel appeared at the top of the stairs in her nightgown asking. "What is it? Is the house on fire?"

Only Ben remained calm. "If you're looking for the Stamps, they left yesterday evening while we were out. They cleared their room. I checked last night; there's not a thing left of theirs, not even a paper tissue," he told the police.

"How do you know that?" I asked a second later.

"Because I saw the note before Dad did. I always knew there was something wrong with them."

I sat on a chair in the kitchen wondering what it was like to be the Stamps, forever on the run, while Dad showed the police out and Mum put the kettle on to boil. "We shouldn't have taken them. But they did pay in advance and we were so hard up I couldn't refuse," she said.

"But never again," I answered. "Never ever, please Mum."

"I wonder whether they've taken anything," suggested Ben.

"The police say we're to check everything. Apparently Tony Stamp is well known to them under the name of Terry Blackstone," said Dad returning to the kitchen. "He has been sent to prison three times for theft."

"Oh no," cried Mum. "And he's been staying here. How awful."

"I'm so sorry for the boys, no wonder they always seemed on their guard," I said. "They were probably expecting the police to turn up."

James and Lisa were still sleeping upstairs. The rest of us discussed the Stamps and drank tea in the kitchen, while day broke outside, all pink and yellow, with birds singing in the tall trees.

"People don't usually pay cash, that should have put me on my guard for a start," Mum said.

"We had better see what's gone," suggested Dad sounding resigned.

So we checked everything valuable; but miraculously nothing was missing.

"They must have liked us after all," said Ben, because some of our ornaments are quite valuable, and they would have been easy enough to steal."

"It's funny how we knew from the start they were wrong somewhere, at least I did," I cried.

"Has Dad checked the money from the fête? Oh my God, where did he hide it?" cried Ben suddenly. "I bet he's forgotten all about it, oh sugar, I bet it's gone and then we will be in the soup."

We found Dad shaving and of course he *had* forgotten all about the money and now we were in turmoil with Bob running about barking madly imagining some sort of game. Dad seemed very slow. I think he had drunk a little too much the night before, which was why Mum had driven home. After several seconds he shouted, "Oh God where did I put it? I can't remember." Then he rushed to the chest in the hall with us following him at high speed with Bob in the rear still barking and Lisa and James rushing about in their night things shouting, "Whatever is it now? What's all the fuss about?" But of course no one had time to tell them. Dad pulled a pile of cushions and old curtains out of the chest and there was the money still in the tin.

And this is really where my story ends. For the money was banked and Gillian caught her flight to the USA on time and months later returned cured.

And as we had the Meacher's house in Corfu to ourselves, Richard and Virginia joined us there, and Ben found himself his first girlfriend ever, and Mum and Dad walked about holding hands saying that it was their second honeymoon. Poor Lisa looked rather left out. Sally, who turned out to have horsey qualifications, looked after Bob and the horses while we were away.

124

And though I grew to like Richard more and
more, we never got further than holding hands,
perhaps because, as Lisa says, I'm very backward
when it comes to boys.

When at last we returned home, the rooms
above the stables had become bedrooms with marvellous beams and a bathroom and loo. But my
room was just the same, and it was wonderful to
know that it was mine as long as I wanted it,
that I would never have to give it up for guests
again.

The horses welcomed us home, while Bob ran
round and round in circles barking with joy.
There wasn't much of the summer left now, but
somehow it didn't matter any more, because our
worries seemed to have been swept away like
autumn leaves. Soon Dad stopped selling double
glazing and became fully occupied supervising
the additions to Black Pony Inn. Mr Meacher
visited us in a chauffeur-driven car from time to
time, his grey hair always immaculate. As for
myself, I wandered about in a happy dream thinking how life might have been with no Lorraine
and no more Black Pony Inn. Instead I seemed to
be living in paradise, and all because we had
decided one July day to help someone who was in
the shadow of death. (And, as Mum says, there
must be a moral there somewhere.)

We never saw the Stamps again. But Mum
visits Colonel Hunter regularly in his new home.
Miss Steele and Mrs Tomson write from time to
time and seem to like living in Oxford. As for the
rest of us, time moves on and we're all changing,
but the summer when we held the fête will

always remain a milestone in our lives, a time when great things were accomplished at Black Pony Inn. A summer when our fortunes changed for ever.